bet

Worshipped Series
Book 2

BRIE PAISLEY

Revised in 2020

Cover art by Arijana Karčić from Cover It! Designs

Edited by Nikki Reeves from Southern Sweetheart Author and Book Services

Formatted by Brenda Wright of Formatting Done Wright

Karen

Staring out of the window, as we get closer to Josh's home, my thoughts race with no end in sight. Feeling out of control and on edge, I glance at Josh, as he lets go of the steering wheel, once the car is parked in front of his rental house.

I've only been out here a handful of times, and to be honest, I'd rather not come here. The house is in a secluded area, and there aren't any neighbors around. It's surrounded by trees, and given the moonless night, it makes the area seem even creepier. The only beacon of light shines from the lone street light, and even then, I can barely see anything.

Josh was silent the entire way here, even though I had asked so many questions, because I don't understand what's happening. Riley, Isaac, and Conner finally told us what's going on with Dominic, only an hour before, and as soon as Riley finished retelling me everything, Josh wanted to leave. Of course, I protested, because I needed to stay and be there for Riley. It's clear they were in turmoil, but Josh wanted us gone.

All he had to do was whisper a demand, that I've secretly come to love, and I had no choice but to leave with him. I don't think we're involved, but his actions are making me question his motives.

Now, we're still sitting in the car, as Josh continues to ignore me. He won't even look in my direction, and my anger is building. Needing answers, I push down my unease with how out of control I feel, and then, I turn to him.

"If you don't start talking, I'll get out of this car, and then walk home. I don't care how far it is from here. I also don't care, if you come after me, but I will fucking leave."

He quickly turns towards me with a look that I'm unfamiliar with, and he also seems annoyed, but he still doesn't say a word, as he gets out of the car. The slam of the door makes me jump, and I lean back into the seat, wondering what he's doing, as he walks inside the house. I can't even begin to figure out what's going on with him.

If only he would talk to me.

A few moments later, Josh walks back to the car, carrying a bag. My heart thumps in my chest, and I get a sick feeling in the pit of my stomach. *Something isn't right*. Unbuckling my seat belt, I get out of the car, and Josh suddenly stops, as he sees me, and then drops the bag. Wondering if he can sense the panic rising inside of me, I slowly move away from the car, but my eyes never leave his.

"Josh, what's going on?"

"Get back in the car," he demands in a tone I've never heard from him before.

Sure, he can be dominant in the bedroom, but he's never demanded that I do anything like this. Alarm bells start going off in my mind, and deep down, I know something is very wrong. Choosing to trust my instincts, I don't think twice about it, as I run away from him. Hearing a curse from behind me, I push myself to run faster.

Darkness surrounds me, as I run blindly into the woods. Vines and tree limbs hit me across the face, as I swing my arms wildly in front of me, trying to block their assault. Stopping behind a huge oak tree to catch my breath, I lean my back against it, trying to blend in. Luck is on my side, since it's pitch black out here, and I never thought I'd welcome the darkness.

The crunching of dead leaves and the cracking of sticks makes me suck in a breath, as I try not to make a sound. "Karen, come out now! You can trust me. I won't hurt you."

His voice is closer than I thought, and I will myself to stay where I am for a bit longer. Taking a deep breath, as his footsteps move away, I peek my head around the tree. Even though I can't see, I do it again on the other side. Thinking Josh is far away now, I back away from my hiding spot, but as soon as I start to turn, I hear him behind me.

"We have to leave. Now."

My entire body tenses, hearing his voice, and it sends chills down my spine, but not in fear. For whatever reason, my body refuses to believe he would hurt me. My brain, however, is screaming for me to run again. Doing what any sane person would do, I run as fast as I can. I only get a few feet away from him, before he grabs me by the arm. He pulls me forcefully to him, and I fall right into his hard chest.

"What are you doing? Let me go!" I yell, but my plea is ignored.

He stills for a moment, and just as I think he's going to do as I ask, he jerks me up, tossing me over his shoulder. While a part of me loves that he's taking control, my rational self won't stand for it. Thrashing wildly and punching his back with my fists, I scream at the top of my lungs.

"Scream all you want, but no one will hear you." He states, and then slaps my ass. Ignoring the instant pleasure that rushes through me, I still fight him. It's who I am, and I'm not giving up without a fight.

"Stay still," he orders, smacking my ass again, while tightening his hold on me. Knowing my fighting is futile, I will myself to relax in his arms. I just need to wait for an opportunity to escape him.

Refusing to let the dark part of myself like what Josh is actually doing, I scream out, "Let me go, you son of a bitch!"

He doesn't say a word, as he stops by the car, and then slowly lets me down. Sucking in a deep breath, as I feel every inch of his hard body, I push the thought of how much I enjoy him manhandling me away. The second my feet touch the ground, I try running again, but he instantly grabs me by both arms, holding on tightly.

He must have known what I was planning.

Looking back, the street light hits his face in such a way, that it stops me in my tracks. His jaw is clenched shut, making his features look harsh, and he takes in deep breaths, as if he's trying to calm himself. With wide eyes, I keep my gaze on him, as leans me against the car, and then opens the door. My heart pounds against my chest, because if I get in the car, I have a feeling he's never going to let me go.

Take control. Get it back.

"Let me go right now, Josh," I demand in the hardest tone I can manage.

"No," he declares with a smirk.

Clenching my jaw, I use every ounce of force I have to push him back, trying to get around him. Against my efforts, I'm pushed back against the car, and my breath rushes out of me.

"Don't try that again," he threatens darkly. His hand reaches up to caress my face, but I jerk away from him. "Don't fight me, Karen. We're going, whether you like it or not." The tone in his voice is absolute, and I know my opinion on the matter is gone.

Hearing the squeaking of the door, as it opens, I don't make it easy for him to put me inside the car. Watching closely, as he locks the door, before shutting it, I don't even get a chance to escape, before he's inside the car.

Holding in a curse, Josh stills for a moment, seeming to regain his composure. I've never seen him like this before, and my stomach drops, feeling the tension inside of the car. His hands grip the steering wheel, until his knuckles turn white, as his breath comes out in pants. Swallowing hard, as I continue to watch him, he closes his eyes almost as if he is looking for some sort of inner calm.

When he finally turns towards me, for a split second, I get a glimpse of him behind his mask. My heart begins to race, knowing I've never seen that look from him before. Josh has always shut me out, when it comes to anything to do with his past, and now, I fear whatever he's hiding, it's not anything good.

"I'm so sorry, Karen. This isn't the way it was supposed to go," he claims in a hard tone.

Frowning, all I can do is stare at him, wondering what the hell he's talking about. "What the fuck is happening? This isn't the time for secrets and to be vague." Sucking in a breath, I will myself to calm down. "Just tell me what's going on. Please," I say, almost on a whisper.

When he opens his mouth, I think for just one second that he's finally going to confide in me. However, his jaw clenches, and then I feel something stinging my arm. Looking down, I realize that he injected me with something. Snapping my gaze up, I try to tell him how much *I hate him.*

Even though anger rushes through me, whatever drug he's injected me with is taking over. Blinking my eyes, Josh becomes blurry, and no matter how hard I try, my eyes start to close.

As I fade out, I hear him say, "I'm sorry. Please, forgive me."

Waking up sometime later, I feel like my mouth is jammed full of cotton balls. My head pounds, as I sit up, and then I run a hand down my face, trying to fight the grogginess. Wondering why I feel like utter shit, I realize my thoughts are foggy. *Why can't I remember anything, before this moment?* Letting out a moan, when my head pounds again, a hand lightly touches my face.

Immediately jumping away, I slowly open my eyes, seeing Josh sitting beside me. "What's going on?"

At first, I don't understand why he looks so worried and sad maybe? He quickly masks his emotions from me, before I can decipher them, and then, I glance around the room, realizing none of it is familiar. "Where are we?"

When he continues to ignore me, I close my eyes, fighting through the pain to remember. After a few moments, it all rushes back. Snapping my eyes open, I jerk my head towards him, holding back a groan in pain. "You drugged me," I claim through clenched teeth. Something flashes across his face, and for a moment, fear races through me, but then, it's quickly gone, and I wonder if I imagined it. "Why?"

My anger flares, when he turns away from me, and it's clear he's not going to tell me anything. Pushing out a breath, I ask, "Can I have a glass of water?"

He nods, and then leaves to go get it for me. While he's gone, I look around the room again, trying to get a hint of where the fuck I am. It's so hot and humid inside this cheap hotel. It also smells like dirty feet, and the walls seriously need to be repainted.

The TV looks like the one that my grandparents had, and it even still has bunny ears on the top. Turning my gaze towards the two beds in the room, I instantly want to move off the one I'm sitting on. The bedding looks worn, feels scratchy, and needs to be bleached. I don't even want to see what the bathroom looks like.

I need to get out of here.

That thought quickly dies, as Josh returns with the glass of water, and I take it from him without a word. Watching him, as I drink the entire glass, he stares right back at me. *What is he thinking*? I can never tell, since his moods change faster than I can think sometimes.

He watches me closely, as I finish the water, and I swear he looks proud. These drugs are having a weird effect on me, because I shouldn't like that look. Choosing to ignore it, I set the glass down, and then sit up straighter. *It's time to get some answers.* "I need you to tell me what the hell is going on. I need answers, and you will tell me," I say, with the most demanding voice I can muster.

He smirks, and before I realize what he's doing, he's right in front of me. Our noses are almost touching, as he asks, "Do you really think you're the one in charge here?" I stay still because that tone … it's doing something to me, and it's also scaring me a bit. "I suggest that you keep your fucking demands to yourself. I'll tell you, when I'm ready." A breath quickly leaves me, as he reaches up, grabbing the back of my neck. "You will do, as you're told."

His tone of voice tells me all I need to know.

He's in charge, whether I like it or not.

Unable to gaze into his dark, brown eyes any longer, I drop my gaze. I've only seen him like this a handful of times, and even then, it was only in the bedroom. Josh has this way of controlling me, even when I didn't know he was. A part of me likes it, but the other part, is full of apprehension. What if I can't get through his thick walls? What if he loses control? *There has to be some way for me to get him to talk.*

He's still inches away from my face, and I can't stop myself from taking in his intoxicating scent. His breath smells like cinnamon, and I realize I'm giving into him. Shaking out of his grip, I back away, leaning against the headboard. Lowering my head, I don't want to meet his intense gaze. If I do, all of the fight in me will vanish. My face flushes, and I know it's red.

Fuck me.

I don't understand why I'm embarrassed, but I am. I don't want to like the way he makes me feel. It was never like this before, and I can't help but wonder *why now*. It's almost as if he's turned into a different person, and with the way my body is reacting to him, it scares the shit out of me.

I shouldn't like him acting this way.

Swallowing down the lump in my throat, as Josh places a finger under my chin, I slowly glance at him. His dark eyes gaze into mine, and it's as if I can feel his need for me. Using his thumb, he rubs my chin, and it sends delicious chills all over my body. I know he cares for me, or at least I think he does, but I still don't understand why he took me. I want to know why, but I also don't want to push him.

Holding back my questions, as he caresses my face, he moves his other hand to the back of my neck again. He grabs me, hard enough to get my full attention, and then pulls me forcefully to him. My hands land on his chest, so I don't fall on him, and I notice he's breathing hard.

"I'm keeping you safe, so do as I say and don't push me again. Next time, I won't be so nice about putting you in your place. Now, I want you to take a shower, and then we'll eat. Maybe afterward, I'll tell you why you're here." He lets me go with a little shove, and I waste no time, rushing towards the bathroom.

Shutting the door behind me, I'm grateful there's a lock. Placing my back against the door, I clench my jaw, as so many emotions race through me. Quickly shutting my eyes, as I feel tears building, I inwardly curse Josh. *This isn't like me.*

I'm not this type of woman, because I'm so much stronger than this. I've never ran away and hid behind closed doors. I'm most certainly not the type of woman that cries over a man. I haven't shed a single tear in such a long time, not since my older sister died, and I can't help but wonder, why I feel the need to do so now.

God help me, I don't know what's come over Josh or me. He's never grabbed me like that before. No one has ever put their hands on me the way he did. I'm shocked, but I don't know what I'm more shocked about. Is it the way he acted, or is it the fact that I *liked* it?

Shame fills me, because I shouldn't like what he did. I shouldn't want him to do it again, and I most definitely shouldn't be turned on by it. My entire body is screaming for a release, and I wonder, if I would be acting this way, if we hadn't already been together, before all of this. Shaking my head, I try to clear my thoughts.

I need a plan, and I need it fast. I have to get out of here, before Josh seriously hurts me, or I give into whatever ... this is between us. I don't trust him anymore, and with the way my body is betraying me, I barely trust myself.

The funny thing about all of this is, I thought I was falling in love with him.

But how can I let myself love him, when it's clear he isn't the man I thought he was?

Chapter 2

Jason

Watching Karen, as she races towards the bathroom, my chest clenches, knowing I've scared her. It's not my intention to frighten her, but I need to show her that I'm the one in control. For far too long, I've held back my dark side, and with each day, it's getting harder and harder to pretend to be this person that I'm not.

My job of pretending would be so much easier, if she wasn't so goddamn sexy and mouthwatering. Every single piece of me, craves her, and I probably could have more control, if I didn't want her, as much as I do. She just doesn't realize how much I want to mark her, claim her, and have her pretty lips around my cock.

Clenching my jaw, I stare towards the bathroom, holding back the urge to break down the door, and then fully claim her. I need to leave, before I completely lose control and hurt her. Honestly, I'm surprised I've held back from doing so already, but deep down, I don't *want* to hurt her. It's shocking to say the least, realizing that she's the only woman I don't want to hurt.

Getting up, I grab my keys to my piece of shit car. Giving one final glance towards the bathroom, I shut the door, hoping Karen doesn't get any bright ideas to try and leave. She has no clue we're in Texas, and she'll get lost in this part of town. I chose it for that very reason. No one looks twice at someone like me, nor will anyone call the cops, if they hear a gunshot or someone screaming. Plus, I'm running low on money, and I need to grab more from Frankie.

Sweat begins to form on my forehead, as I walk outside, and then get inside of the car. Summers in Texas are hot and humid, but I've actually missed the heat. Turning the key, the car spurts to life, and I push out a breath, hating how things have turned out. A part of me hates that I had to resort to drugging Karen to get her here, but she gave me no choice. There was no way in hell she was going to leave willingly, but I have to do everything in my power to keep her away from Dominic. I'll kill him myself, before I ever let him near her.

The night I met her, I was completely caught off guard, once I saw her. I didn't expect to instantly want her, and I sure as fuck didn't expect to *keep* wanting her. My only mission was to set up a way to learn more about what Isaac and Conner were up to, but after seeing Karen, the plans changed for me.

I'm not a good man, but I had to save her from a very painful death, because I know what Dominic has in store for her. I don't even question why I've done what I have, because I'm not ready to face it. I don't do right or wrong, but Karen is innocent, and I couldn't just stand by and watch her life drain from those pretty, brown eyes.

Shaking those terrifying thoughts away, I can't bear to go down that road. It brings out every demon I battle with daily, and it makes me think of my dark past. It also makes me realize what kind of monster I really am, because if it weren't for me, another innocent woman would still be alive. However, my past will never allow me to be normal.

Doing what I know best, I shove all these thoughts away, getting back to the task at hand. I need to meet with Frankie to get my money, and then grab food. Pulling out my phone, I dial Frankie's number.

"What do you need, my man?" He answers, after the first ring.

"We need to meet, since I'm running low on funds. Meet me in twenty minutes, and we'll make the exchange." I don't wait for his reply, as I hang up.

Quickly sending him directions in a text, I know he'll show up exactly, as I demanded. He doesn't have a choice in the matter, since I saved his ass a few years back. Dominic didn't make it easy on me, after he realized I'd covered for Frankie, when a drug deal went sour. One thing I've learned in this life, is to always call in favors and only trust myself.

Making it to my destination, I back the car into an alley, and then I quickly get out to pop open the trunk. Grabbing my favorite gun, I tuck it into the waistband of my pants. I don't expect trouble, but it's always a good idea to be prepared. Not to mention, this part of town is dangerous. It's full of want to be gangsters, hookers, and of course, drug dealers.

My eyes scan the area, wishing Frankie would hurry the fuck up, so I lean against the car, and then cross my arms. I don't want to sit and wait, because every time I have a free second, I'm thinking about Karen. I have no idea why she means so much to me.

I don't love her.

A man like me can't love another person, but fuck, she's so much more than I expected. I love how short her hair is, her cute button nose, and her luscious lips. And that fucking ass of hers ... I can't wait, until I leave my hand print on it. I want her ass nice and red for me and only me.

I know she'll enjoy it, because she's already proven how much she likes my demands. All I have to do is pay attention to her body, and how she physically changes, when I do the things I want.

She was made for me.

Shifting my weight, I have to adjust myself. It never fails, because all I have to do is see or think about Karen, and I'm willing to do anything to be inside her. She's different somehow, but I haven't figured out why just yet.

A pang of guilt washes over me, as I think about my past again. *Rachel.* The one that I got killed for being stupid. I didn't feel the same way about her, as I do for Karen. I wanted to care about Rachel in that way, but for some reason, I just couldn't. *Fucking hell.* I have to stop all these thoughts from surfacing. There's no way I can be in control, while thinking about the fucking past.

Finally, Frankie's Ford Ranger pulls up in front of me, and then he gets out. He looks around, as if he thinks he's about to get jumped. *Good.* The little shit needs to stay on high alert, since I have no idea if Dominic knows I left town with Karen or not. I'm hoping for the latter, because if he doesn't, it'll definitely buy me some time to get my shit together. And hopefully, I can get Karen on board soon. If not, I have a plan B.

Walking over to Frankie, I ask, "Do you have it?"

He nods, and then turns to open the door of the truck. He pulls out a large duffle bag, and before he hands it over to me, he glances around the area again. It's good he's aware of our surroundings, but I'm in a hurry, and he's taking his sweet ass time. "What is it, Frankie?" I question, as he hesitates to hand over the money.

"It's nothing, man. Just wondering, why you need so much money."

Jerking the bag out of his hand, I try to reign in my anger. "It's none of your business. I call, you answer, and then come wherever I tell you. Got it?"

"Yeah," he rushes out. "If you're in some sort of trouble, I have your back."

"Good. Now, get the fuck out of here." He quickly turns to leave, and I don't move an inch, until he's out of sight. Frankie has never let me down, but the kid is just that … a kid. Even if he's grown up a lot, since the last time we did a job together, I still don't fully trust him.

It's not in my nature to trust a soul.

Opening the car door, I toss the bag of money in the back, and then get inside. Checking my surroundings, I make sure no one is nearby, before pulling out, and then head towards a store I spotted by the hotel. I'm not sure how long Karen and I will stay here, before going to our next destination, so I only plan to grab the essentials for now. I can't risk staying at this particular hotel more than a few nights, before moving on, and I need to decide, if I'll take her to Mexico. I want her to be on board with going, since it's my home away from all this bullshit.

Maybe, if I tell her what's really going on, she'll want to go, since it's the safest place we can lay low.

If I do tell her about the things I have done, I'll have to be straight with her, and totally honest about it all. The thought of telling her everything doesn't sit well with me, because I was trained to keep shit locked down tight. I can at least start by telling her that my name isn't Josh.

I hate it, when she calls me that.

Either way, once I get back to her, we're going to have a conversation about all of this. One way or another, she'll agree to my terms.

It's just a matter of time.

Chapter 3

Karen

Hearing the hotel door shut, I let out a sigh of relief. I give myself a moment, before I decide to open the door, making sure Josh left. Swallowing down the lump in my throat, I slowly open the bathroom door, and he's nowhere in sight, so I know it means that he's gone.

For now, at least.

Pulling the door open further, I forget all about having a shower, hoping he doesn't decide to come back any time soon. I need luck to be on my side for just once today. If he comes back, before I'm gone, this entire plan to escape him will be all for nothing.

Walking out of the bathroom, I move towards the room's window, and then pull back the disgusting curtain. Once I realize Josh isn't standing outside by the door, I glance back at the room. I've never been more grateful that I don't have any belongings. It'll be much easier to make a quick getaway without a heavy bag, dragging me down.

The only thought that crosses my mind, as I slip out of the hotel room, is getting the hell out of here. Quickly scanning the parking lot, a rush of adrenaline flows through me, as I realize Josh's car is missing. With my heart pounding in my chest and ears, I start walking, not really knowing which way to go. I have no idea where I am, and my only plan is to get as far away as possible. It's the only thing on my mind right now, and it's a struggle to stay at my pace, instead of running, like my body is telling me to do.

However, I don't want to have any attention drawn to me, because how odd would it be to see a woman, running in jeans and a t-shirt? Not to mention, I probably look as lost as I feel.

Finally making it out of the parking lot, I turn right, heading down the main road. Every step gets a little easier, and my confidence grows, thinking that I've gotten away. Traffic becomes heavier the further I walk, and a after a few moments, I turn to the side, hoping I can flag someone down to stop and give me a ride. Sweat rolls down my back, making my shirt stick to me, and it coats my forehead, as I try to get someone's attention.

The heat is unlike anything I've ever experienced before, and I'm not sure how much longer I'll be able to stand it. My mouth is so dry from lack of hydration, and I fear I'll die of a heat stroke or dehydration, before a soul stops to help me.

Waving my arm at a black car, hope blooms in my chest, as the driver pulls up to me. The driver rolls down the window, asking if I need a ride, and then I nod, thanking the man for stopping.

Not once, do I think about what the stranger might do, or who he is. All I'm thinking about is getting the hell out of the heat. The cool air from within the car is a welcome relief, because my health is the priority. Everything else gets pushed to the back of my mind.

The driver seems nice enough at first glance, and he doesn't seem to be putting off any killer vibes. *Then again, what do I know?* Josh seemed like a nice guy, too. My judgement in people is off, since I don't get out much. I'd much rather work or be at home, watching a movie.

Once the man pulls away from the curve, I ask, "Can you take me to the police station, please?"

He doesn't say anything in return, but I take it on blind faith that he'll take me there. For a while, he drives around for a bit, but then, I notice he doesn't get on any main highways. Instead, he keeps turning down back roads, and frankly, I'm starting to get a bad feeling about this. It shouldn't be taking so long to get to the police station. Even if I'm not familiar with the area, I know something is off. What's even creepier, is the guy hasn't said a word, since I got into the car. He just holds onto the steering wheel, staring straight ahead.

Panic starts to take over completely, as he purposely misses the turn for the highway. When he passes by two more exits, I start becoming more aware of my surroundings. Although I don't know my way around this area, I know the empty streets he's turning down isn't a good sign. Seeing a gas station, I open my mouth to ask him to stop, as he passes by it. However, my heart sinks, realizing it's out of business. My instincts are screaming at me to get out of this car, as we pass by more abandoned buildings.

Turning towards the driver, I ask, "Can you stop here? I can walk the rest of the way."

He glances at me, and my stomach drops, when he slowly smiles. "We're almost there."

"Please, just pull over."

"Just relax," he says, trying to pacify me, but panic is the only thing I'm focusing on.

My heart races, and I get a sick feeling in the pit of my stomach, as he steals quick glances at me, while he continues to drive. There are no signs of him stopping and dread consumes me.

"Where are you taking me? I want out now. Stop the car," I demand loudly.

"Don't worry, doll. We're here," he claims, as he parks the car.

Jerking my gaze towards the window, my breath catches in my throat, seeing where he's taken me. The house, what's left of it anyway, is barren, and everything about it comes off as wrong. There's a huge red symbol on the side, and I know it means something. It makes no sense to have that symbol on the house, and it's clear no one has lived here in a long time. Is this a place where drug dealers come to sell drugs, or could it be something more sinister?

I've made a grave mistake, getting inside this car, and the second I realize my mistake, my entire body reacts. Trying to keep calm and not alert the man, I slowly reach for the door handle, as I say, "Thanks for the lift."

As soon as I grab a hold of the door handle, the man grips my wrist tightly. "Now, where do you think you're going?"

"Let go of me!" I yell, trying desperately to jerk my hand away. Using my other hand, I hit him on his shoulder, doing everything I can to get his grip to loosen. His fingernails begin to dig into my skin, and I let out a scream, as he jerks me to him.

"Don't you worry, doll. We're going to have a lot of fun together," he sneers in my face, and I use my free hand to push him away. It's no use though, and I fear I won't be able to break free of his grasp.

Right as I'm about to attempt to get away from him once more, the driver side door is forcefully jerked open. With wide eyes, I suck in a harsh breath, seeing Josh on the outside. *How in the hell did he find me?* God, his eyes are dark and void of any emotion, and a rush of fear races through me.

"Let. Her. Go. Now." Josh demands through clenched teeth.

"She's mine. Go find your own whore," the driver claims, and my temper flares, hearing him call me that.

Despite my anger, I don't get a chance to retort back to the whore comment, as Josh grabs the man by the throat. I'm suddenly free, and this is my one opportunity to escape. Reaching for the door, I barely get it open, before Josh orders, “Don’t fucking move an inch.”

The tone of his voice scares me, but it also excites me. *What the fuck is wrong with me*? I should be running far away from him, but I find myself sitting back against the seat. Honestly, I’m too shocked at how he’s reacting, and I can’t seem to pull my gaze away from him. He pays me no mind, once he realizes I’m not going anywhere, and then he turns back to the driver.

Watching carefully, I frown, as I notice Josh’s grip on the driver’s throat is hardening. His hand is turning white from the strong grip, and the driver’s face is turning blue. “Stop! Let him go,” I plead.

Josh doesn’t even spare me a glance, and I don’t know if he’s even listening to me. “Josh, please. You’re going to kill him.” The driver doesn’t have long left, but he hasn’t given up yet. He fights against Josh’s hold, but it’s clear that it’s futile. “Please,” I try once more.

Finally, Josh’s eyes meet mine, and for a second, he holds my gaze, before jerking his hand away from the man’s throat. Relief flows through me, because I don’t want a man to die. As a doctor, I took an oath to do no harm and to help others. Acting on instinct, I reach over to check the man’s pulse just to be sure his heart rate is returning to normal.

It’s clear he’s struggling with catching his breath, but honestly, I don’t feel sorry for him. Even if he’s coughing harshly, I don't feel an ounce of sympathy. As soon as my fingers touch his throat, I'm jerked forcefully out of the car. Snapping my gaze to the right, I pull back, seeing Josh's angry expression. In the back of my mind, I know it's useless to fight him, but I try anyway. He jerks me again, and I almost fall out of the car with how hard he's pulling my arm.

"Don't make me hurt you, Karen," he states in a deep voice.

God, his voice.

That deep and commanding voice does something to me. As if I'm in a trance, I instantly stop fighting, and then I willingly get out of the vehicle. I don't say a word, as Josh's grip on my arm tightens, and he all but drags me towards his car. Without a single word, I'm placed inside the vehicle, and I cross my arms, as he shuts the door. Watching, as he walks around the front, a thought crosses my mind, making me suck in a breath.

If he really wanted to hurt me, wouldn't he have done so by now?

If he doesn't care for me in some way, then why is he going through all this trouble, just to keep me by his side?

My gaze stays on him, as he gets inside the car, and I'm not sure what to think about all of this. I wish he would just tell me the reason why he's doing this, but I hold back my questions, knowing he won't tell me. Snapping my gaze away, I jump, when he slams the door shut. My heart pounds in my ears, as he sits quietly, and I stare straight ahead. It's as if I can literally feel the anger, rolling off of him in waves, and I'll admit, I'm a bit scared of how he's going to react.

Once he starts the car, I suck in a calming breath, and then ask, "Why did you come after me?"

I don't expect him to answer, but I'm surprised, when he says, "You're safer with me."

"What does that even mean?" I ask, as I face him.

He doesn't say anything for a while, as he sits, staring out of the window. The tension in the vehicle intensifies, and I shake my head, thinking he's going to ignore me again. After a few moments, his jaw clenches several times, before he asks, "Do you understand the danger you put yourself in?"

Deciding not to answer, I glance down at my crossed arms. "Do you have any idea what that red symbol on that house meant?"

Again, I choose to stay silent. In my defense, I hadn't expected the guy, that picked me up, to be such an asshole. I also have no idea what the symbol means, but I have a feeling Josh is about to enlighten me.

His voice deepens, as he claims, "You would've prayed for death after him and his buddies were finished with you. That symbol …" he stops, and I glance up, seeing him pointing towards the house. "That symbol is what men like him use to let others know they can fuck you, even without your permission. It's his job to bring beautiful women here for the sole purpose of getting paid, while others rape them."

Dropping my head, I try to swallow down the lump that's suddenly lodged in my throat. "I … I didn't know," I whisper.

"Yeah. That's pretty fucking clear, so do us both a favor, and stop fucking running from me."

Turning my head, I look out of the window, as Josh drives away. Leaning back against the seat, I let his words replay over and over in my mind. If it weren't for him, I could be inside that house, right now, being raped again and again. If it weren't for him, I would've completely lost myself, and I probably wouldn't have ever come back from that. Yes, he did save me, but why do I still feel the urge to run from him?

Can I really allow myself to stay with him, knowing it's going against everything that makes me, me, or am I just fooling myself, and I'm really not the person I think I am?

Jason

While driving back to the hotel, I think long and hard about what to do with Karen. *She's going to keep running.* It's not in her nature to give up this much control, even if I know there is a side to her that desperately wants to. It doesn't matter what I have to say on the matter, because I see the uncertainty written all over her face, as well in her body language. Karen is the type of woman that won't fully trust me, unless I do something that I've never done before.

She'll keep trying to escape me, unless I tell her everything, including all of my secrets and about my past.

I've never told a sole about it, and I don't think I'll be able to open up about it to her, either.

I'm surprised I actually told her about what would happen to her, if I hadn't found her when I did. Honestly, it was pure luck I happened to spot her, getting inside that piece of shit's car. I should've known she'd try to run, and I won't make that same mistake again. The fear that overcame me, once I realized what she'd done, shocked me to my core. The only emotion I feel is anger or rage, and the need to spill blood.

Fear was beaten out of me.

Nevertheless, I felt it for the first time, realizing she almost slipped through my grasp.

At first, I thought Dominic had found us, and then took her away from me. Rage unlike anything I've ever experienced before overwhelmed me, but as I begin to tear apart the room, I realized Karen had left of her own free will.

Glancing over to her, I try to let my anger go. It's difficult, because I want to kill the man she was with. Not only for taking her, but for laying his hands on her. Smirking, as I turn my gaze back towards the road, it gives me great pleasure, knowing I'll be back later for him.

He will pay for his crimes.

Arriving back at the hotel, I'm pleased, as Karen shows no resistance, as I lead her back inside the room. I plan on punishing her for putting herself in danger, but the vixen before me, has another agenda. As soon as I shut the door, she doesn't spare me a glance, as she quickly rushes towards the bathroom.

Running a hand down my face, I remind myself that I have to be patient with her. However, I'm getting really sick and fucking tired of her running off, and then completely shutting me out. I want nothing more than to make her beg for a release, as I make her ass red with my hand. I want her to tell me she'll stay by my side, because that's where she belongs. I want her to willingly submit only to me, and I crave hearing those sweet words, coming from her lips. I never thought I'd want to hear such ridiculous words from her, but I do.

I want every single piece of her.

Instead of bursting into the bathroom, I decide giving her privacy is the best course of action. Karen is stubborn, and she's unlike any woman I've come across before. I can't deny that there is something about her that calls to my dark soul, and I'm smart enough to know that it means something. If she were any other woman, I would've already done everything I wanted to do, since the moment I met her, and then forgot all about her.

For some reason, I'm holding back. It's shocking that I've done so without slipping, but after today's adventure, I know she's seen the real me. However, she's only witnessed a fraction of what makes me, me.

Pushing out a breath, I get up and start to pace. Karen is taking too long in the shower, but I know she's still in there. The small bathroom doesn't have a window, so my little escape artist can't get past me unnoticed. Moving closer to the door, I hear that the water is still running. It makes my cock hard, knowing my woman is behind the door naked and wet. My need to see and touch her is overwhelming. These intense emotions, she brings out of me, are something I've never experienced before, and at times, I don't know how to handle them.

I have a feeling it'll always be this way with her.

Not giving myself a second more to change my mind, I slowly open the bathroom door. Holding back a groan, as I see her behind the clear shower curtain, my eyes roam her naked body. *Jesus fucking Christ.* She's the most beautiful woman I've ever laid eyes on. My entire body is primed and ready to claim her, as I watch her slowly run a hand down her perfect tits.

Standing still, I'm torn between what to do, as she uses the same hand, and then runs it down her stomach. Her hand only stops, once it's between her legs. A part of me wants nothing more than to watch her make herself come, but the other part of me, the demanding and dominant part, wants her to stop.

While I try to figure out which part of me will win out, my eyes never leave her perfect body. God, it's as if she was made for me and only me. Licking my lips, as her head falls back, I have a sudden urge to be the one to touch her. I want to be the one to make her feel pleasure, like she's experiencing.

Knowing which side has finally won out, I take two steps towards her, and then jerk the shower curtain open. She startles, as she notices me, and then her face turns a bright shade of pink that I've come to love, seeing on her smooth skin.

"What the fuck are you doing?" She asks, breathless.

Glancing down, I smirk, seeing that she hasn't removed her delicate, little fingers from her tight pussy. Without a word, I reach down, and then pull her hand away. She moans, and I suck in a deep breath, enjoying the sound. Looking back up, I hold her gaze. Keeping the hand, she used to fuck herself, I grasp it tightly, while I use my other hand to cup her hot pussy.

"This," I say with a hard tone. "This is mine." Karen's eyes widen, and her eyes dilate. I'm sure she doesn't realize how she's inching closer to me, or how her pussy begins to drip with her essence. She loves it, when I show her my true self. "Your pleasure will only come from me," I demand.

Her lips part, as she takes in a deep breath, and I bring her fingers to my mouth. My eyes never leave hers, as I suck them clean, and then I groan, as her taste hits my tongue. Pulling them free, once I'm satisfied they're clean, I claim, "You taste divine, vixen."

"Please," she utters in a small voice, and I know exactly what she's asking for.

"No," I snap back, because I don't think I can hold back my darker urges with her.

She's not ready to see who I really am yet, and I know she only wants me now, because she didn't get the release she wanted. "No more touching yourself. Do you understand?"

"What if I don't give a fuck what you want, and then do it anyway?"

Smirking once more, she's bound and determined to test me. "Do it, and you'll see exactly what I'll do."

My threat hangs between us for a moment, but I feel how wet she's getting from it. "Lie to yourself all you want, vixen, but your body tells me everything I need to know." Even if I don't want to move my hand, I do, and then reach down to turn off the now cold water.

Grabbing a towel off the rack, I wrap it around her, and then begin to dry her off. Feeling her gaze on me, I state, "You like it, when I'm this way."

I don't meet her eyes, but I know she's confused. I wouldn't expect anything less, honestly. In a different life, maybe I could've been a nicer guy, and someone who deserves Karen. However, this is the reality we're in, and I'll take her, whichever way I can.

Once she's dry, I help her out of the shower. Finally, I let myself gaze into her light, brown eyes, and I was right. Confusion is laced in her gaze, but I don't know how to explain myself. I just wanted to care for her in my own way, but the words to tell her that refuse to come.

"I don't understand you," she whispers with a frown.

"I know."

She's not the only one confused, either. All of the emotions, running through me, are puzzling. I know how I was trained to feel, but when I'm around Karen, I experience sensations I've never felt before. Unable to decipher through them, I suck in a deep breath, and then I pick her up.

Carrying her to the bed, I let her fresh scent fill my nose, before setting her down. She holds the small towel that's wrapped around her tightly, and for a split second, I actually feel regret for what I'm about to do. It should stop me from going through with it, but it needs to be done.

Until I can trust her, this is the only way I know she'll stay by my side.

Her gaze follows me, as I slowly walk backwards to my bag on the other side of the room. It's smart of me to have her in my sights at all times, because knowing her, she'll up and run on me again. Reaching down to grab my bag, I open it to find what I need, while never leaving Karen's eyes. Pulling out the handcuffs, her gaze drops to them for only a second, before meeting my gaze again. She's not going to like this, but I don't have any other choice. She's safest with me, and I'm the only one that can protect her.

Whether she wants to admit it or not, she needs me.

Walking back to her, she swallows hard. Hearing her suck in a breath, I remind myself to keep calm, as she pleads, "You don't have to do this. Please, Josh. Don't do this."

Taking ahold of her wrist, she fights me, as I place the cold metal on her. "Don't make me hurt you," I claim, as she continues to fight against me.

I don't want to hurt her at all, at least not this way, but I will if I have to, to make my point clear. She relents with a sigh, and I quickly snap the handcuff to the bed.

Satisfied she's not going anywhere, until I release her, I step back. She jerks her arm to test the strength of her new bonds, as she asks, "Why?"

"It's the only way," I utter, before turning around, walking back towards my bag.

"I fucking hate you," she sneers.

Clenching my jaw, I turn back to her and tilt my head. "I really don't give a shit, if you do or not. I'm doing everything I can to make sure you keep breathing, so do us both a favor, and get with the program. You've already put us in more danger than before, so I would suggest you do as I say, without your fucking attitude."

Shaking my head, I'm angry at myself for going off on her. Karen just knows how to push me to my breaking point, and I know it's because of her control issues. Turning my back to her once more, I quickly grab my things, and then head to the bathroom.

The cold shower will surely cool off my need for her, or at least, my anger.

Chapter 5

Karen

Clenching my jaw, I let out a string of not so nice words, as Josh retreats to the bathroom. I'm so angry with him, my situation, and mainly, for him handcuffing me, like some common criminal. Jerking on my wrist, I will the bed to be frail. Giving up, once I realize it's useless, I move closer to the headboard, trying to get comfortable. Glancing down at my wrist, it's starting to turn red from all of the pulling.

All of this because I tried to get away from him.

It's ridiculous and insane he's going to these lengths to protect me. *Or so he says*. I wonder if he's going to keep me handcuffed to the bed the entire time, or will he resort to some other method? Crossing my legs, I squeeze them together, trying to relieve the ache that's still there. *God, help me*. I can't help my body's reaction to Josh, and honestly, I don't mind the handcuffs.

I shouldn't *like* this.

I shouldn't *want* this.

Fuck. What's happening to me? The moment Josh took me, I knew deep down, that something had changed between us. I'm not sure how I know. Maybe, it was my instincts, or maybe, I knew all along that Josh isn't just a normal guy. Now more than ever, I don't know, if I regret meeting him.

My thoughts come to an abrupt halt, as I hear the water shut off in the bathroom. Clutching the towel with my free hand, I can't seem to look away from the door. I'm not afraid of him. No, it's just the opposite. It feels like anticipation, and I wonder if he's still angry at me for running and defying him. My emotions feel as if they're all over the place, and I suck in a heavy breath, trying to get it under control.

But nothing, and I mean nothing, prepares me for when Josh walks out of the bathroom.

With my heart pounding, I lick my lips, as I take in his muscular form. He's naked, and still wet from his shower. Seeing the water, running down his sculpted back, I have a sudden urge to lick him dry. It's not fair that he looks so edible, knowing I'm supposed to be pissed at him for kidnapping me, and then handcuffing me to the bed.

No matter how angry I am, I can't take my eyes off of his body. My eyes track his every move, as he walks over to his bag, and I have to bite the inside of my cheek, holding in a moan, when he bends down. A man like Josh is a devil with an angel's perfect body, and that thought makes my breath rush out.

Noticing the scars, covering his back, legs, and shoulders, I wonder where he got them from. As he stands, his dark hair falls in his eyes, and I wish I could brush it out of his handsome face. Josh hasn't even bothered to look in my direction, so I take it as my cue to continue gazing at him.

He turns, and when he does, my eyes widen, as I get a full up and close look at the tattoo on his left arm and on his side. I've seen it before, but for some reason, he never let me examine them like this. The tattoo on his arm is a full sleeve of what looks like an angel facing down with a sword, or some sort of weapon in its hand. On his side, it looks like a devil, or demon facing upward. It's as if the two are battling each other.

Whatever it means, it's a big tattoo. The angel takes up most of his shoulder, and some of his middle back with its wings. The devil covers his left side completely. When he turns to face me, I glance at his chest. His other tattoo isn't anything spectacular. It's just a simple name in cursive writing.

Julian.

I don't know anything about Julian, or if it's a man or a woman. Josh has never been very open about his past, and I learned that fact very quickly, when I asked him about this particular tattoo.

Thinking back to that night, I remember instantly regretting it. It was the first time I realized that he had a darker side, and it was the one and only time that I begged him not to leave. Something about his behavior scared me, and the moment he got dressed, I feared he'd never return.

What I remember most about that night was the look in his eyes. They were dark, cold, and full of hatred. His entire body was tense, as if he was preparing for a fight. I didn't understand why a simple tattoo had brought out such anger from him, but I tried to get him to open up to me.

But no matter what I did or said, he still left me anyway.

Coming out of my memory, when he sits down beside me, I secretly thank him for putting on some clothes. The less distracted I am, the better off I'll be, especially if I'm going to try and get some answers out of him. For a moment, I just gaze at him, wondering if his mood is better.

My fingers start to twitch, seeing the scruff on his face, but I will myself to stay still. His dark eyes never waver from me, and I swallow hard, before asking, "What am I doing here, Josh?"

Glancing away from his gaze, I can't stand to look at him any longer. It's not out of fear, but it's more of how intimidating he's being. Somewhere deep down, I *like* knowing he can *make* me submit. Shaking my head at the direction of my thoughts, I raise my head and square my shoulders.

"I can't stay here, and you and I both know that. I have my job, friends, and someone is going to start looking for me, when I don't show up for work." *Or when I don't call Riley tomorrow.*

Riley and I have talked every single day, since the moment we met, and if anyone suspects something happened to me, it'll be her. For a fleeting moment, I think he's actually considering letting me go. His eyes soften, as he pushes out a breath, and I lower my voice, pleading once more. "Please, Josh."

The second those words leave my mouth everything changes.

His eyes are no longer understanding and comforting. Now, they're full of anger, and I clutch the towel tighter than before, when his jaw begins to clench. I can literally feel and taste the rage, coming off of him in waves, but I don't understand what pissed him off so quickly. I shrink back, as he leans over to me, but again, it's not out of fear. I don't know why, but I know he won't hurt me. *At least, not physically.*

He grabs me by the chin, and I stare into his dark eyes, as he claims, "You. Are. Mine."

Each word is spoken with such finality, and I have no other choice, but to believe him. "I always keep what's mine, so you'll stay by my side at all times." As my lips part to take in more air, his gaze drops to them. My entire body feels like it's humming with a sexual need for him to dominate me even more. "Everything is taken care of, so there is no need to worry about your job."

His thumb traces over my bottom lip, and I think over what he just said. My mind is in a fog, but I desperately try to shake it off. Even with the smooth and calm tone of his voice, there is something about what he just said, that makes a sudden surge of anger wash over me.

Shaking out of his grip, I ask, “What did you just say?”

He sighs, as if he knows what’s about to happen. “I paid someone to call and leave a message, explaining where you’ll be for the time being. I’ve also arranged an email to be sent, letting the right people know to send in your fill in to cover for you at the clinic. I’ve taken care of it all.”

With each word spoken slowly to me, as if I’m a child, I frown, trying to get a handle over my emotions. But no matter how hard I try, anger fuels me, as I let what he’s done fully wash over me.

“This. Is. My. Life!” I yell, wishing I was free, so I could push him away. “How dare you fuck with my life! How dare you jeopardize everything I’ve worked so hard to build. You have no right to do any of this.”

Feeling the heat on my face, I know the rage building inside of me is showing, but I don’t give a shit. As much as I love hearing him claim me, I cannot sit by and let him control me this way.

“This isn’t right, and you know how much my job means to me. How could you do this to me?” Shaking my head, I state, “I wish I’d never met you.”

My words must hit a nerve somewhere in him. His eyes turn cold, and before I realize what he’s doing, his hand is around my throat. His grip isn’t tight or hurting me, but it’s enough pressure, to let me know he’s in charge. My face flushes once more, and I wish I had more control over my body. In my mind, I know this is wrong, but my body *loves* this side of him. It’s never been clearer to me that something about us isn't right, as I arch my chest towards him, *begging* for more.

Quickly stopping myself, I clench my jaw, as he says, "I would never, ever fuck with your career. Your place at the clinic will still be there, when this is all over. Do not ever assume anything with me. Do you understand?" His grip tightens, and I relish the feeling of his fingers, digging into my skin.

What is wrong with me?

Why am I enjoying this?

"I told you," he continues, as if whatever he's doing to me is completely normal. "I'm doing this all for you. Everything I've done has all been for you."

My heart beats hard and fast in my chest, as his eyes roam down my body. Goose bumps begin to cover my entire body, as he slowly takes me in. I'm only covered by a small towel, and I lick my lips, wondering if I should let it go.

Once his eyes meet mine again, he huskily says, "I'm going to take off the handcuffs, so behave, and I'll reward you."

Reward me? Josh doesn't give me time to ponder on what he said, before reaching over, and then unlocking the cuff around my wrist. Now that I'm free, I suck in a deep breath, thinking over everything that's happened.

There is only one option here, if I'm going to come out of this fully sane.

Standing by the bed, I spot a metal lamp on the bedside table out of the corner of my eye. Before I give myself time to think about what I'm about to do,

I quickly reach for the lamp, while Josh is distracted by my half nakedness. Using all the strength I have, I hit him on the side of the head.

He grunts loudly, as he falls off the bed, and I'm shocked I actually did it. Not sparing him another glance, I take off running out of the door, clutching the towel in my hand. I don't dare look back, as I race through the parking lot. I don't let myself worry about only wearing a towel, or that I have nothing to aide me.

I just know I need to get away from Josh, before I give into him, and let him take over me completely.

Jason

Groaning, I touch the tender wound on my head. “Fucking hell.” Ignoring the pain, I stand, as quickly as I’m able, and then glance towards the door. It’s wide open, which means my little vixen is running.

Again.

Clenching my jaw, I will myself to stay calm. I will the beast within to back the fuck down, because this shit is getting old. Finally standing tall, I shake my head, trying to focus on the here and now. It’s hard fighting through the pain, racing through me, but I push past it.

It’s what I was trained to do.

Using the back of my hand, I wipe the blood that’s sliding down the side of my face. Not sparing it a glance, I race out of the room, and then scan the parking lot for Karen. Out of all the times she chooses to run, this shouldn’t have been it. She’s not thinking rationally at all, and when I find her, I’m going to make sure she knows not to ever leave my side again.

It doesn't take me long to track down my clever escape artist.

Once I have her, I ignore all the bullshit coming out of her mouth. I don't dare look at her wild, brown eyes. All I care about is getting the fuck off the streets, and back to our hotel room.

"You son of a bitch! Let me go, you psycho! I hate you. I fucking hate you!"

Pulling her hard by the arm, I almost falter, when I hear her whimper. Pushing past the unfamiliar twinge of guilt, I walk her closer to our room. Thank fuck she wasn't any quicker to get away from me. Finding her, hiding behind a dumpster, was just lucky, but then again, I think she knew she had nowhere else to go. Either way, I have what's mine now, and no one, and I mean no fucking one, is going to keep her away from me.

Not even her.

I keep what's mine.

"I can't believe you would do this to me," she tries again. "I thought we had something, Josh. I—"

"If you know what's good for you, then you'll shut that pretty fucking mouth up." Glancing down at her, I smirk, seeing the anger in her eyes. "What? Got something you want to say?"

She opens her mouth again, but I tighten my hold on her arm, daring her with my eyes to disobey me. After a few tense seconds, she relents, looks away, and then I guide her into the room. "That's what I fucking thought." Slamming the door shut behind me, I sit her down on the bed. "Don't move."

Feeling her eyes on me, I walk to the sink, and then check over my throbbing head wound. Using my fingers, I gently touch it. Fuck it hurts, but I'm glad I don't need stitches. Letting out a sigh, I grab a hand towel, wet it, and then clean off some of the dried blood around it.

As I'm cleaning my newest wound, my eyes meet Karen's in the mirror. I hold her gaze, because she needs to see that I'm still here, and that I'm proud of her for doing whatever was necessary to protect herself. Yes, it fucking hurts my ego that she used her newfound head bashing skill against me, but at the same time, I know she can handle herself, given the chance.

When she glances away, I toss the towel down, and then turn around. Crossing my arms, I suck in a deep breath, considering my options. Karen is a very stubborn woman. When I first met her, I knew she was hiding who she really is underneath all that made up bullshit.

She thinks she's the dominant one, but she's far from that.

She's a submissive.

The only problem is, she's convinced herself that she's always in control, but deep down, I know she desperately wants someone to control her. Although she and I never had this conversation, any dominant male would see right through her. Maybe, she's met all the wrong men. Maybe, they were all a bunch of pussies.

All I do know is, shit is about to change.

Whether she wants to admit she likes it or not.

With my mind made up, I decide I'm done playing the good guy for her sake. I'm done being fucking *Josh*. I'm done being the lie Dominic wanted me to play.

Walking over to her, her eyes meet mine, and I want to smile, seeing the excitement staring back at me. "Stand up," I command.

She hesitates, and it's only for a moment, but she does comply. Reaching up, I take her small hand, and then move it. The action causes her grip on the towel to falter, and it falls down onto the floor. Holding her gaze, I slowly let her hand go, willing myself to stay in control. It's harder than I thought, knowing this beautiful woman, standing before me, is completely naked and vulnerable.

She's waiting for me to do whatever the fuck I want with her, and it's intoxicating. Wanting to see how far she'll let me go, I drop my gaze. My eyes slowly travel down to her plump breasts, and I suck in a deep breath, as her nipples harden. Clenching my hands, I force myself not to palm both of those generous breasts. Moving my gaze down, I take in her lean form, all the way down to her pink pussy. Lingering there for a moment, I swallow, remembering how good she tastes. Finally, my eyes take in everything, even her feet and toenails, that are painted a fire red.

My cock is straining hard in my pants, but I ignore that need. There is something else I need, and it's something she needs just as bad. "Turn around."

Once she does as I've commanded, I take a seat on the edge of the bed. As I devour that perfect ass with my eyes, I use my hands, moving her exactly how I want her. I'm impressed she hasn't fought me, but then again, she knows I'm in control.

"Bend down and hold your ankles," I force out, once I have her standing to the side. She frowns at my demand, and I tilt my head to the side, as her gaze meets mine. "Do it now, Karen."

After a moment, she lets out a breath, and then gets into position. Having her like this in front of me, is driving me insane with the need to fuck her just like this, but I remind myself that we both need what's coming. Now, that she's exactly where I want her, I reach out my hand and ever so slowly, slide it up her leg, and then to her thigh. Hearing her breath quickening, I stop once I reach the underside of her ass cheek. Holding my hand where it is, I glance at her.

"What are you doing to do to me?" She finally asks, and I smirk.

"Everything you need me, too," I answer right as I come down hard on her ass, using my hand.

Karen

The pain is the first thing that registers.

"Don't fucking move," he demands, as I try to get away from his hand. Doing as I'm told, I shut my eyes, willing myself to stay where I am. Another loud smack, lands on the already tender spot, and I let out a … moan?

That can't be the sound I heard, but yet, I feel myself, moving *towards* him and his hand.

As he lands another blow and then another on my ass, it turns into something … more. It hurts yes, but it also feels good. Actually, it's better than good. It's turning me on, making me want his fingers, mouth, or his cock.

I want him to fuck me, like his blows are landing.

Hard.

Rough.

Punishing.

He pauses for a moment, and I open my eyes, hearing his breath rushing out. "Please," I beg.

His hand gently rubs my ass, and I'm sure it's turning red. "Please what?"

"More." As soon as the word leaves my mouth, he delivers. "More," I ask again.

Every single time his hand lands on my ass, my entire body instantly craves another. This shouldn't be turning me on. This shouldn't be making my pussy clench with want and need. This should definitely not make me want this every single chance I can get.

After two more blows, my legs begin to shake, and then he pauses again, slowly rubbing my tender cheeks. "No more running, Karen. Do you understand?"

He smacks my ass, wanting me to answer, and I swallow, before saying, "Okay, I won't run again."

Another smack. "Admit you love this. Crave this. Need this," he demands of me. *Smack. Smack.* "Say it, Karen." *Smack.* "Say you need this from me."

Smack.

Smack.

Smack.

"Yes! Yes! Yes, I admit it." Fuck, it's starting to really hurt now. I've passed the point of pleasure, and it's as if he knew I was getting there, too.

"Good girl," he coos, as he relaxes me.

"What did you do to me?" I ask, because this isn't normal. This isn't me.

Is it?

Josh doesn't answer, but he does guide me to stand. Watching him, as he crosses the room, he opens his bag, grabs something, and then walks back to me. Unrolling a shirt, he helps dress me, and I wince, as the fabric touches my tender ass cheeks.

Surprisingly, he caresses my face, and I frown. This isn't a side I'm used to seeing, either. I get the half nice Josh, or the one that with one look, I think he might kill me. This Josh is throwing me off, but I feel pride, rushing through me. It's almost as if this is my prize for being good and doing what he wanted.

It shouldn't feel like this, and I shouldn't fucking like feeling this way.

"What did you do?" I ask again.

His hand drops from my face, and I blink away the confusing emotions, racing through me. How can I hate him, but at the same time, want to please him? How can I want him to touch me, but yet, punish me for running?

"I only did what you wanted me, too."

"I didn't ask for you to beat me," I sneer.

"Watch your tone," he barks back, and I suck in a deep breath. I have to remind myself who this man is, even if I'm confused about what's going on with me. "No, you didn't ask me to *spank* you. You needed it. Just like I needed to do it to you."

Shaking my head, I step away from him. "No. No one wants to be spanked. No one wants to be beaten, like a dog."

Even as the words leave my mouth, I know I'm lying. "You're lying to yourself, Karen." *Great. Even my captor knows I'm a liar*. "Remember how you felt, as I gave you what you needed."

As his words roll around in my mind, he guides me back to the bed. Dazed and lost in my own emotions, I don't fight him at all, when he sits me down, and then handcuffs me again. The pain from his brutal blows hurts more than I care to let on, but I don't mind it. It's a reminder of sorts, but I don't let myself think about it longer than I have to.

It's not normal to like the burn …

God, I'm so fucked up.

"I have to go take care of some things." Josh says quietly, as if he's testing me.

Glancing up, I meet his dark, brown eyes. Holding his gaze, I suck in a deep breath, knowing that it's pointless to argue. I'm already handcuffed again, and he isn't the type of man that will back down.

"Alright." Shock registers across his face, but only for a second. If I hadn't been watching so closely, I would've missed it.

He nods once, and I watch him closely, as he crosses the room to grab a bag. As he heads towards the door, I call out to him. "At some point, you know you're going to have to tell me what this is all about."

He doesn't glance back, or even acknowledge that I've spoken. However, I know he heard me. "Also," I add, and then take a deep breath. "I'm sorry for hitting you with the lamp. I never wanted to hurt you." Yes, I wanted to escape, to gain my freedom at all costs, but I never wanted to hurt him.

I can't be sure why my statement makes him turn around. I may never understand anything about him, but the look in his eyes, makes my stomach drop. It's the look of someone who's lost an instrumental amount in their life. A man that has nothing left to give or to care for. He just looks … lost.

"That's the thing about people, Karen. In the end, no one wants to do anything to hurt another person, but we do it anyway, because we have, too."

Josh has been gone for a long time.

I know this because of two reasons. One, the clock on the night stand tells me so, and two, because dawn is approaching. No matter how hard I tried, sleep evaded me. There are a number of reasons why I couldn't find sleep, but the main one is that I'm worried about Josh, and if he's coming back.

It's stupid to want someone like him. After everything he's put me through, I shouldn't *still* want him. No matter how hard I try to convince myself that it's wrong that I feel this way, it doesn't change a thing. So, while I've sat and sat alone with my thoughts, I decided I really don't care anymore about right or wrong.

I feel the way I do for a reason, and that's that.

My decision is confirmed, as soon as he walks through the door. I'm falling hard for him, whether I want to or not.

My heart pounds in my chest, seeing he has come back to me, and for a moment, I feel glad. But then, he turns around, and I see the blood, and the emptiness in his eyes. Swallowing hard, I force myself to stay calm. I remind myself that maybe there is more to this than what I'm seeing.

"What happened to you? Are you hurt?" My stomach suddenly forms a huge knot, making me clench my jaw even thinking about him being hurt. Fighting the urge to pull at my restraints, I wait for his answer.

Josh finally glances down at himself, as if he's just realized he's covered in blood. He frowns, as he locks gazes with me, and then he says, "It's not mine."

Relief like I've never felt before, rushes through me, but then, I frown. "Who … whose blood is it?" God, why did I ask that? Do I really want to know?

"No one that matters," he states, as he drops a duffle bag on the floor.

Swallowing the sudden lump in my throat, I quietly ask, "Did you hurt someone?" His shoulders slump, as if he knew the question was coming, but he doesn't answer me. "Josh, please tell me what's going on here. Tell me you didn't hurt someone else."

Even as I speak, I know what his answer is going to be. I've known who he really is all along, even if he hasn't said so. It's a feeling, like a sudden realization, that he's not who I thought he was.

His dark eyes meet mine, and I suck in a deep breath, knowing that everything is about to change. My heart drums rapidly in my chest, as Josh sucks in a breath, and then says, "I didn't hurt anyone, Karen." Closing my eyes, I relax, thinking this was all a misunderstanding, until he claims, "I killed someone."

Fuck. He just admitted to murder.

He just told me he killed someone, not in self-defense, but *murder*.

Opening my eyes, I stare back at the monster, and I realize, I still feel the same way about him.

I'm still falling in love with him.

So, what kind of person does that make me?

Jason

I can't believe I said the words out loud to her, even though I refuse to admit whose life I took. The bastard that tried to take her from me had it coming anyway.

Admitting the truth about who I am, was easier than I thought, but now, here comes the hard part. The part where she'll react just like the last woman I thought I cared for did.

She will fear me, and the monster that I am. She'll be disgusted at the man I've become, and she'll refuse to have anything to do with me. Waiting for her reaction, I think about how I wish that I were different. I also wish I didn't feel the urge to hurt anyone.

Unfortunately, it's the one thing I'm good at, even if I want to stop. Even if I want to change and not fill this dark void with every person's life I take, I know deep down, it's not possible. Yes, I fight like hell most days to keep this evil side of me at bay, but it's getting exhausting. Since meeting Karen, some days are easier, but I know I'm fighting a losing battle.

Even if I could be different, only for her, I wouldn't know where to begin.

I don't know how to be … normal.

I've been this way for as long as I can remember. The dark side has always been there, waiting it seems, to break free, ever since I was a child. My childhood was not … right. I don't know if that's the sole reason why I am the way that I am, but I do know, it played into it.

I know Dominic also played a huge role in how I grew up. Maybe, if my mother hadn't sold me to him at fourteen, I might've had a fighting chance at normalcy. Shaking away those unwanted thoughts, I push away the memories of Dominic. I bury those horrific days of 'my teachings', as he liked to call them, away. I want to burn away every single memory of me being forced to do things that no one could ever imagine.

I want to rip out the memory of me being the one to hear Caroline's screams, when her father burned her alive for helping Isaac and Conner.

"Josh?" Clenching my jaw, I fight against the beast within, as it claws inside me. "Josh, what's wrong?" I can hear and smell her, so I fight harder for control.

God, help me.

I don't want to hurt her.

"Josh, it's alright. I'm right here, and I'm not going anywhere."

Backing away, I turn, and then head straight for the shower. I don't waste time washing the blood off of me, because for once, I'm desperate to get it all off of me. Once I'm finished, I quickly dry off, dress, and then remind myself to stay calm. The beast within is present than usual, so I have to be careful.

After minutes, or fuck hours it feels like pass, I regain full control. The monster is still there, waiting for its turn to take over, but it's calmer, almost pleased in a way. Focusing on Karen, once I walk out of the bathroom, her gaze never wavers, as I move towards her.

Pulling out the key to the handcuffs, I quickly free her, and then stand back far away from her. A part of me is … worried that I might hurt her, so distance is my only option. She still doesn't look away, as she rubs her wrists, and I get the urge to pound my chest, like a fucking cave man. Pride is something I haven't felt in so long.

Truthfully, any emotion has evaded me for … years it seems. Until the moment I laid eyes on Karen, all I felt before was emptiness.

"Are you alright now?" Frowning at her, I literally don't know how I should answer. Instead, I stay silent. "Josh?"

God, that fucking name is like nails on a chalkboard. "That's not my name," I correct her with more anger than intended. Her eyes quickly dart away, and I'm a fucking bastard for liking that, too.

"We should talk," I ease out, hoping not to fuck this up any more than I already have.

Her shoulders fall, as if she's dreading having this conversation, even though we both know it needs to happen. Giving her a few moments to prepare for what I'm about to say, I walk closer, needing to be near her. My dark beast is slowly easing up, even more than before, so now, I feel more in control over myself.

Just as I reach her, she glances up, and then asks, "What's your real name?"

"Jason Hamilton."

"Why lie about your name?"

"It's complicated," I say with a gruff voice.

Her jaw clenches, and I know she's not happy with that answer. No matter how badly I want to confide in her, I still don't trust her. It's not in my nature to trust anyone, and sadly, she's no different.

"What's the point in talking, if you're not being honest with me?" Her question is valid, however, what I need to tell her isn't going to go over so well.

Taking a seat beside her, I lean my arms down on my legs, as I admit, "You're in danger, Karen."

As I look back at her, wanting to see her reaction, she frowns, as she asks, "From who?"

Seeing no point in lying to her anymore, I glance away, as I admit, "Dominic."

Once the name leaves my lips, she jumps up, and then begins to pace in front of me. Clenching my jaw, I know she's starting to put all the pieces together. That's one of the things I like most about her. She's smart as hell, so it won't take her long at all to fill in the blanks.

"You know him," she grits out, but I don't answer her. When she finally stops pacing, she turns to face me, as she states, "You're working for him."

"Yes," I confess, even though she didn't ask for an answer.

"Why?" Her eyes narrow, as she adds, "Does he have something over you?"

That hits too close to home, so instead of giving her another piece of me, I stand up. The urge to walk away is so strong, because it's difficult to face this part of myself. I never wanted her to know what kind of man I am. I never wanted her to see how easy it is for me to end someone's life.

No matter what I've done, I never wanted her involved in this.

"I told you it's complicated, Karen."

Anger flashes in her gaze, and I'm not surprised about it. I wouldn't expect anything less, honestly. As we continue to stare at one another, I watch, as she finally figures out the truth. It's all present in her eyes, as she realizes what I've done.

It's even clearer, as she steps back, and then clenches her fists by her sides.

"I was your way in. That's why you were so concerned about Riley and her life. That's why you wanted to be around me." I know better than to utter a word, as she works through it all, but it's hard not to defend myself. "You used me to hurt the one person I love the most."

Giving into my inner most needs, I step towards her, but she holds up a hand, as she demands, "Stay away from me."

"No," I snap, because she doesn't get to run away from me. "I told you that you're mine, and I meant it."

"I don't give a damn about what you say anymore. You're nothing but a fucking liar, and a master manipulator. You used me. You lied to me."

Understanding, suddenly washes through me, and I let out a sigh, realizing I've done more harm than I thought. She's clearly upset that I was working for Dominic, but she's more upset, because I hurt her by doing so. I have no doubt that she cares about her friend, but as a woman, she's devastated about what I've done *to her.* Judging by the pain in her eyes, she thinks she means nothing to me. I'm sure she thinks the entire time, when we were together, was nothing more than a lie, too.

I may have lied about my name and hidden my intentions, but when I was with her, it was real.

It all was.

Reaching my limit of staying away from her, I take another step, and then grab her arm. Pulling her to me, she fights me, just like I knew she would. I take each of her hits against my chest, knowing she needs to get it all out. Karen is the type of woman that doesn't do anything she doesn't want to, so I know this fight she's putting up, is nothing more than her way of working through things.

Wrapping my arms around hers, I pin her to me, and then, I wait for her to submit. She may think of me as a bastard, but she doesn't have the full story yet. I'm still not sure if I should tell her about my son, or my childhood, or fuck, even why I stayed with Dominic as long as I have, but she needs to know that what this is between us isn't a lie.

Unfortunately, Karen still fights against me, and I'll admit, I'm losing my patience. It's hard to keep myself under control, knowing the dark side wants to overtake me. Which is why I know, if I don't get her to stop and listen, I will slip.

I could kill her so easily.

Knowing how easy it would be, I fight even harder against my nature.

It's the fear of hurting her that gives me the strength to keep calm.

Jerking her back by her shoulders, her hand breaks free, and then she slaps me across the face. Using my tongue, I touch my bottom lip, tasting blood. A smile crosses my face, as surprise crosses hers.

"You want to play, then?" I grit out.

Her jaw clenches, and even if she's still angry, I know she's also turned on by what she's done. It's so present in her gaze, and I won't lie, just seeing her desire, turns me on even more than before.

Closing the distance between us, I make sure to take her wrists, and then place them behind her back. "Don't hit me again," I demand. I don't think I can keep holding back, if she keeps fighting me so hard.

"Get away from me," she snaps, but I ignore it, hearing how breathless she is.

Leaning down, I whisper, "You don't want that. Not really."

"Fuck you."

Smirking, I use my teeth to bite her earlobe, and Karen sucks in a harsh breath. Giving into my need for her, I begin to kiss the side of her neck, and I know she's loving every second of it. Her chest starts to press against me, as if she's seeking more attention.

Deny it all she wants, but I know my vixen wants me just as much as I want her.

Using my free hand, I slip it under her shirt, loving the soft moans she lets escape. God, I love the feel of her soft, smooth skin against the palm of my hand, and my cock hardens, as I reach her plump breasts. Pulling her breasts out of her bra, I handle them roughly, mainly because I can't do fucking sweet and gentle anymore.

Sucking on her neck, I know I'm going to leave a mark behind. I don't care if I do, because I want everyone to see it. I've never been a possessive man, but when it comes to Karen, I want to own every single inch of her. I want to claim her in ways I never knew even existed before.

As another moan leaves her lips, I take her mouth hard, devouring everything there is about her. She doesn't even bother to fight me anymore, and the moment she melts in my arms, I slowly let go of her hands. The instant I do, I tense, waiting to see if she'll push me away.

She doesn't.

Her arms wrap around my neck, and I guide her to lay down on the bed. Taking her hands, I place them above her head, and her brown eyes gaze at me, curiosity laced in them. "Don't move," I order, and I know she likes my command.

There is still defiance in her gaze, but she stills, like I demanded. Licking her lips, my cock jumps, wishing I had those hot, wet lips around my cock. Taking her mouth once more, I ignore the sting of the cut on my lip from her hand. If anything, it makes our kiss even more pleasurable.

As I taste her, one of my hands slowly begins to run down her side. I don't bother, taking my time at all, mostly because I can't fucking wait, and neither can she. There will be other times to tease her, but not now.

Once my hand is on her stomach, she pulls away from my mouth, taking in a deep breath. Pushing my hand down, I stop right as I touch her clit. The move makes her buck against me, as a loud moan leaves those pretty lips. However, I don't move just yet.

Using my other hand, I grab her chin, making her look at me. "You. Are. Mine. Don't ever forget that, Karen."

The fire in her gaze burns brighter, but she also knows I'm right. It's clear she knows there is no going back now, and as if she accepts that, she slowly nods her head, as her jaw clenches.

The moment I feel her submit, I slide a finger inside of her. She's so wet and hot that it makes me groan, along with her throaty moans. Clenching my jaw, I will myself not to lose control. I want nothing more than to fuck her raw, until we're both so exhausted, that we can't even move. However, I know deep down, she's not ready for that.

She's only had a taste of the real me, so I remind myself to take it slow.

If I don't, she'll end up resisting me even more than ever before.

"Please," she cries out, as I continue at my slow pace.

Adding another finger inside of her, her hips rotate, trying to make me move faster. Smirking, I lean down to bite her lip, as I thrust into her deep. My pace is still slow, because I want her out of her mind with lust.

Only then, will I give her what she wants and craves the most.

Letting go of her lip, I move back to her neck, kissing and sucking the spot I know she loves the most. Her loud moans fill my ears, and it's like the purest music I've ever heard. Using my thumb, I begin to rub her clit, and I know she's getting close to orgasm, as I feel her tight walls, clenching around my fingers.

Biting her hard on the side of her neck, she cries out, and I thrust inside of her hard. “Please, please,” she begs, but I need more from her.

“Say my name,” I demand, wanting to hear it come from her lips.

I know she’s fighting me, when she turns her head away, but I won’t allow her to defy me this time. Stilling my fingers, her head snaps back towards me, and her eyes are wide with frustration.

“Give me what I want, vixen.”

Her jaw clenches, but I know she’s close to giving in. With my thumb, I use it to rub circles on her sensitive clit, but I refuse to move my fingers. “Say it, Karen,” I command in a deep voice.

“Please, Jason, make me come.”

Nipping at her jaw, I give her the reward she’s wanting. Fucking her hard and fast, using my fingers, I bring her right to the edge, waiting for that moment of bliss to cross her beautiful face. It doesn’t take more than a few thrusts, before she’s calling out my name, and her pussy is clenching around my fingers.

After a few moments, she finally comes down from her orgasm, and I enjoy seeing the pleasure in her brown eyes. She seems perfectly content in this moment.

It’s just a shame that it can’t last.

Chapter 9

Karen

Guilt eats away at me, and I fear I'll never surface from it.

Once *Jason* pulls his skillful fingers out of me, I lay still, wondering if I'm a horrible person. It didn't take me long at all to figure out what was really going on, once he told me that Dominic is the reason why he took me.

I just wish he would've told me that I was wrong.

I hate knowing the truth, even if I feel he's still keeping a lot from me. I'm not sure how I'm supposed to feel either. Should I be angry at Jason for working for Dominic? Should I hate him?

It's hard to get my emotions in order, since they're so conflicting. On one hand, I'm falling for Jason, but on the other, I know I shouldn't be falling in love with him. Right and wrong don't apply here, and the gray areas are everywhere. It's not black and white, or laid out in a perfect order for me to figure out.

I'm all on my own with this, and I don't know what I should do.

Knowing all of this, I hang onto anger most of all. Anger I can deal with, especially since it's placed right where it's needed. I'm so angry that Jason has done nothing but use me this entire time. I still can't believe I'm the reason how Dominic found his way into Riley, Isaac, and Conner's life. A part of me knows I can't be held responsible, but the other part, seems to think I should've known better.

Letting out a sigh, Jason moves off the bed to answer his phone, and I'm glad for the distraction. No matter what I feel, I can't seem to keep my guard up around him. He seems intent on bringing down every single wall of mine without a thought. I know I should be afraid of him, but deep down, I can't seem to find that emotion. Yes, I'm afraid of Dominic and for Riley, but I'm not scared of Jason.

How can I be, knowing he's done nothing, but protect me? I admit, his actions aren't promising, but I know there is something else behind all of this drama. There has to be a reason why he's this way, and why he's working for a madman.

If there isn't a reason, I don't think I can face it.

Getting out of bed, I run a hand down my hair, and then make sure to quickly get dressed. Glancing over to Jason, I get a sick feeling in the pit of my stomach. Whoever is on the phone, it's clear it's not a good call. It's in the way his shoulders tense with every second that goes by, and also, with the way he's looking out of the hotel window. It's as if he's checking for danger, and I swallow hard, thinking he very well could be.

Needing a distraction, I walk towards the bathroom. As I walk inside the tiny room, I stop dead in my tracks, as my appearance catches my attention. Touching my neck, I suck in a deep breath, seeing all the marks on my skin. I knew he was biting and kissing me, but I hadn't realized he was actually *marking* me.

I have to look away, when desire flushes through me.

I don't understand why seeing his marks on me send such delicious tingles straight to my clit, or why I want him to do it again.

Quickly taking care of my needs, I wash my hands, and then walk out of the bathroom. The moment I do, fear is the only thing that's present. Frowning, as I lock gazes with Jason, I know something is wrong.

"What is it?"

His jaw clenches, and then he states, "We have to go. Dominic knows I've left with you."

My heart begins to race, as I work through what he's saying. Licking my lips, I try to fight against the overwhelming sense of fear, racing through me. "What does that mean? Is he coming for us?"

It takes him a few steps, before he's standing right in front of me. He runs a hand through my hair, and the gentleness in his touch throws me off balance. "No one is going to hurt you. I swear you'll be safe."

Gazing into his dark eyes, I know he means what he says. However, it's not me who I'm really worried about. The more I work through what's going on right now, the more I wonder exactly who is going to keep him safe?

Who is going to protect Jason from Dominic's wrath?

Two weeks later

We've been on the move a lot lately. I don't question Jason's need to keep moving, because each time we leave, I see the tension literally evaporate. Even if I know what's going on, I still hate the situation we've found ourselves in.

It also doesn't help that he continues to handcuff me, once we're in a new place. I get it, but it still hurts to know he's so untrusting. I'm smart enough to know, if I were to leave, I'd most likely get myself killed. So, I've kept my thoughts to myself, hoping if I'm complacent, he'll eventually see that I'm on his side.

Watching him from the bed, I can't help but wonder who he's talking to. He's been distracted, since we arrived at this new hotel, and I know there must be something big happening. I know this because he hasn't restrained me yet. It's coming, that I have no doubt about, but I won't give him a reason to hurry up with it.

So, I watch him, as I sit on the bed. The more that he paces the room, the more I worry that we've been caught. Something isn't right with this call, but I have no idea what it could be. I've tried to get him to open up about everything, but no matter how patient I am, he still shuts me out. I won't even admit to myself how much it hurts to know he doesn't trust me at all.

When he curses loudly, and then slams his phone down onto the table, I jump. I'm glad for the distraction, because I honestly don't want to dig further into how I feel. It's easier to push it all down, and then pretend like I'm indifferent.

But I can't ignore the instant rush of adrenaline, when he walks right out of the room, and I quickly realize he left his phone behind. My heart pounds in my chest, as I slowly get up, and then begin to walk over to the phone. In the back of my mind, I know if I pick up his phone and call the one person who needs to know I'm alive, I'm giving Jason another reason not to trust me.

Instead of sitting back down, I watch the door, and then quickly walk over to grab the phone. The need to let Riley, or hell anyone, know I'm alive is too strong to ignore. Glancing back towards the door, I keep my gaze on it, as I walk into the bathroom. Shutting the door, I let out a sigh, seeing Jason doesn't have a lock on his phone.

My heart begins to race, as I dial Riley's number, and my stomach clenches, when it starts to ring on her end. Even if she doesn't answer, I remind myself that it's okay. As long as she knows I'm alive and well, it'll give me some type of comfort.

However, the longer Riley's phone rings, the more nervous I become. I want more than anything to be able to talk to her, and a part of me hopes that she'll let someone know to come find me. While I know staying with Jason might be safer, I can't stop myself from at least trying once more to leave him behind.

"Hello?"

Relief like no other flows through me, hearing Riley's voice. "Riley? Thank God! Josh, I mean Jason, is crazy."

"Karen? I … hear … you … breaking up."

Fuck. I can barely hear her, and I worry that if I can't understand her, then she can't understand me either. "He took me, Riley. I have no idea where I am." When she doesn't answer, I add, "Riley? Riley, can you hear me?"

Frowning, when she still doesn't answer me, I look down, seeing I have no service in the bathroom. Not knowing what else to do, I start to end the call, but before I get that chance, I feel hands, grabbing me from behind.

Letting out a piercing scream, I kick and thrash my arms around, hoping that whoever has me in their grasp, will let go. I know it's not Jason. The hands wrapped tightly around me feel different than his, and Jason wouldn't have grabbed me. He would've demanded to know what I was doing, or at least, turned me around to face him.

As the man drags me out of the bathroom, I still fight him. Fear courses through my veins, as I realize this must be one of Dominic's men. He must have found us, and as soon as the thought forms, another type of fear runs through me.

Jason could be dead.

Or he could be hurt badly.

Knowing he needs me, I use all the strength I have, and then head-butt the man. He instantly lets me go, and I don't waste a second, getting away from him. Racing towards the door, I glance back, satisfaction filling me, knowing the man is hurt. The blood from his nose is running through his hands, and pride fills me, knowing I got away.

But as soon as I turn back around, I slam right into someone else.

Thinking it's another one of Dominic's men, I start to fight again, until I hear his voice. "Karen, it's me. It's alright. No one is going to hurt you."

Glancing up, I meet his dark gaze, and I sink into his open arms. "Thank, God. I thought you were hurt or worse, dead."

He frowns, as he answers me. "I'm fine. Why would you think something was—"

Jason's words are cut off, when we hear a loud groan behind us. Keeping my eyes on Jason, he glances to the guy who grabbed me, and then looks back to me. "What happened?"

The tone of his voice tells me that he's angry, but I'm not sure who he's mad at. Swallowing hard, I state, "He grabbed me, and I broke his nose to get away."

"He touched you?"

Clenching my jaw, I nod, unsure why I suddenly feel, as if I've done something wrong. "Does he work for Dominic? Is he after us?"

Jason's entire body tenses, as he shakes his head, and I know I've fucked up. That's the exact moment the man speaks. "Jason, I heard her on the phone, talking to someone named Riley." It's clear the guy is in pain, since he has yet let go of his nose.

Guilt rushes through me, knowing I caused someone pain. As a doctor, I took an oath to do no harm, so it's hard for me to realize that I didn't hurt him on purpose. I mean, I did, but only to get away from him. In that moment, I wasn't worried about anything other than my own safety, and I wasn't worried about anyone else, except Jason.

"Frankie, tell me you did not fucking touch her."

Stepping out of Jason's arms, I cross my arms, as I glance back and forth between them. "You know each other," I state loudly, as anger rushes back.

"Frankie," Jason calls out, completely ignoring me.

"I didn't know she was going to freak out, but I also didn't think you wanted her to call anyone. If Dominic is tracking your calls, it could lead him right to us."

When Jason doesn't utter a word, I wonder if he's upset that I did call Riley. I hadn't thought about Dominic tracking his phone, and now, I definitely wish I hadn't called her. What if I bring him right to us? Have I doomed us?

"You don't ever touch her," Jason claims, and I frown, as I look at him. Both of his fists are clenched by his side, and I have an urge to touch him.

However, I don't get a chance to do so, as he takes a few steps, and then stops, once he's standing a few inches away from Frankie's face. "What the fuck did I tell you, when I told you to check on her?"

Unsure of what to do, as Jason towers over Frankie, I stand still, worry racing through me. "I wasn't supposed to harm her," Frankie utters in the softest tone I've ever heard. It's as if he's trying to seem nonthreatening, but I don't think Jason is thinking clearly.

The more he stares at Frankie, the more I wonder, if he's going to lose it. The last thing I want is for Jason to hurt Frankie for doing what he thought was right. Walking over to them, I reach for Jason, hoping to settle him.

"Jason, it's alright. I'm fine," I claim, hoping that's enough for him. Even if I don't know Frankie, I don't want him to face Jason's rage. It's clear he doesn't have control over himself, and I don't know, if I can handle, seeing the monster that I know is in him.

"Jason," I try again, when he hasn't even looked my way.

"Don't fucking test me right now, Karen," he says, as his hard gaze lands on me.

Instinctively, I glance down, knowing I can't face the coldness in his eyes. "Jason, man, I'm sorry," Frankie claims, but it's clear he isn't in the mood to hear it.

"You're sorry? You're fucking sorry?" Snapping my gaze up, I quickly realize Jason has wrapped his hand around Frankie's throat. Panic and fear almost overwhelm me, as Jason pushes him against the wall.

"Jason, stop! Let him go," I yell, hoping he'll listen to me.

Frankie surprises me, when he doesn't fight Jason's hold. It seems as if he knows his fate, and he's willing to accept it. However, I'm not willing to back down. Grabbing Jason's arm, I try to pull him off Frankie. "Jason, please stop. You're hurting him."

After a few more tries to get him to let go, it's clear I'm not getting through to him. I know I have to act fast, since I notice Frankie's lips are starting to turn blue, and I know he won't last much longer.

Reaching up, I place a hand on Jason's cheek, pulling him towards me. "Jason, look at me. I'm fine, and you can let him go. He's not going to touch me again."

Jason's eyes slowly focus on me, and relief flows through me, seeing his grip loosening. "That's it. It's alright, Jason. I'm fine, and you can let him go now."

As if a dam brakes, Jason forcefully drops Frankie, and then backs away from us. I make no move to check on Frankie, because I don't think

Jason would appreciate that move. Standing still, Jason glances back to Frankie on the floor, coughing hard, and then back to me.

When he finally gazes back to me, I hold his gaze, and I feel he's trying to tell me something, even though it's clear he can't speak the words. I know this moment is important, although, I'm not sure why, but I don't look away. I can't seem to anyway.

It's only when Jason walks out of the room, I let go of the breath I was holding, and then I make sure that Frankie is alright. Glancing to the door, I look for Jason, and fight against the urge to go comfort him.

The sensation scares me, because if I want to comfort him, what does that exactly mean for me? I know what kind of man he is, and what he's capable of, so if anything, I should want to be free of him.

But I don't.

I want to stay by his side and understand the man that would do anything to keep me safe.

Even if that means, he takes a life to do so.

Chapter 10

Jason

Losing control isn't something I'm familiar with. I learned long ago, losing control the way that I did, can mean the difference between life and death. It can mean your guard is down, and something terrible will happen.

I've seen it once before, and it ended with the mother of my son dying.

I shouldn't have lost it with Frankie. I shouldn't have let the anger and jealousy get the best of me. This is why I hate being around Karen. She brings out a part of me that I thought died years ago, but I'm beginning to see, I only buried my emotions. They're still there, waiting to break free, no matter how hard I fight against them.

A part of me knows the longer I'm with Karen, the more my hold over all the consuming emotions, will break free. A part of me wants that to happen, but the other part, wants to stop it.

I can't be a monster with emotions, clouding my judgement. I can't be the perfect killer, knowing I'll be overwhelmed with guilt and shame. I can't be filled with regrets of my choices or actions. I have to own what I am, no matter the cost.

If I let go of it all now, Karen's life will be in more danger than before.

Sucking in a deep breath, I feel the anger and rage slowly dissipate. Using the techniques Dominic drilled into my head, I get myself under control. The moment I do, I hear someone approach from behind. For a moment, I think it's Karen, but I quickly realize it's Frankie, as he steps beside me.

"I think we should move again," he suggests, and I nod, knowing he's right.

If Karen did call her friend, it could mean Dominic knows our location. Leaving this hotel behind is a good choice. "No hard feelings," I state to him, and he'll understand why I can't actually say the words to apologize.

"No hard feelings." He repeats, and I nod once more, knowing things between us are back to normal.

Or as normal as they can be, between two cold-blooded murderers.

The moment we get to a safer location, I order Frankie to leave. He was only here to provide some backup, when I realized Dominic's men were near, but I know he'll stay close by just in case I need him again.

I might not trust the kid, but he is loyal to a fault.

My old friend, Marcus, is the one who brought him into our world of chaos, and it's the only reason why I trust him to be around. Frankie looks up to my old friend, for reasons I'm not clear on.

Leading Karen into our new room, I watch her closely, as she drops her bag by the bed. Glancing at it, I think back to the moment I realized we needed to leave town. The exact moment Dominic ordered me to get close to her, but I always had a backup plan. I didn't want to be responsible for getting Karen involved, but I didn't have a choice.

The more I got to know her, and the more I spent time with her, I made sure to have everything ready to disappear if needed. Turns out, it was very necessary.

Feeling her gaze on me, I look at her, taking her in. Need courses through my veins, and I know she feels it, too. Her lips part, as she begins to pant. The sexual tension in the room skyrockets, and it hits me right in the chest, making me take a deep breath.

Taking a step forward, I expect her to tense, or even tell me she doesn't want anything to do with me. I hate knowing she saw me become the monster that I know I am, but at the same time, I'm glad she saw. I'm glad she knows exactly what I'm capable of.

So, when she makes no move to stop me from advancing forward, pride rushes through me. Karen is a strong woman. That I have no doubt about, and seeing it right now, just makes me want her even more than I have before.

Once I'm standing in front of her, I reach up, and then brush her blonde locks out of her face. The touch makes her eyes close, as if she's enjoying my gentle touch, even if I'm shocked that I want to be tender with her in this moment.

When she opens her eyes again, our gazes lock, and for the first time in ages, my heart begins to race. There is just something about her that makes my body act like it never has before, and I shouldn't be shocked by it. She has made me feel more than I ever thought possible, especially these past few weeks.

Her brown eyes stare up at me, as I work through all the sensations she brings out of me, and my cock hardens, seeing the desire filling her gaze. I know what she wants, but a part of me needs to hear it.

"What do you want, vixen?"

With a shaky breath, she says, "You. I just want you."

Moving my hand from her hair, I place it on her neck, bringing her closer, as I lean down. I place a kiss firmly on her lips, and the urge to take her mouth harder almost consumes me. The moment she opens her mouth to suck in a breath, I slip my tongue deep inside, demanding her obedience. As she submits, I reward her by cupping her cheek, all the while, kissing her deeper and harder.

It's as if I can't get enough of her mouth and her taste. I'm getting lost in her, but I find that I don't care anymore. I let myself fall deeper in lust, letting all the stress from staying off Dominic's radar, fade into the background. It's easy to forget, when Karen is involved, and that's one of the main reasons why I have to keep her.

She makes it easy to forget the kind of man that I am.

Just as I begin to move my hand down to touch her breasts, the new burner phone chimes with a message. At first, I ignore it, unwilling to stop kissing and touching her, but when I hear the noise again, I know someone is trying to get ahold of me. As much as I don't want to stop what I'm doing, I know I have to.

Breaking our kiss, Karen's eyes are so full of want and need that it makes my cock jump, because I need her just as badly. However, I know whoever is trying to talk with me is probably attempting to either warn me, or it's Marcus with an update.

Right before I walk away from Karen, her hand reaches out, grabbing my forearm. Gazing at her small, delicate hand on me, my stomach drops, wondering if she knows how much I crave that tender touch from her.

"You're not upset with me that I called Riley, are you?"

Understanding rushes through me, and I realize I've kept her in the dark so much that she's right to mistake me pulling away as anger. My eyes soften, as I gaze at her, and then I cup her cheek again, as I say, "No, I know why you did what you had, too."

Her eyes drop, as she confesses, "I put us in more danger by calling her. Not to mention, I've made a mess for her, too."

Ignoring my phone once more, as it chimes again, I sit by her, knowing she needs me in this moment. "If anyone is to blame, it's me." Her gaze snaps to mine, and I can see the confusion in her eyes. "It's my fault you're in this mess, and I feel partly responsible for spying on your friend."

As the words leave my mouth, I realize how true those words are. I do feel guilty about what I've done, even if I know I had no choice. The thing is, it still surprises me that I actually feel this way.

"I know you're only doing this for a valid reason," she claims, as her hand clasps with mine. "You can tell me the truth, Jason."

Looking up, I hold her gaze, knowing she's right. I know I can trust her, and a part of me wants, too. I want nothing more than to let all my past demons free, and then start over with a new life with her. Clenching my jaw, I fight the urge to tell her every sick and twisted thing I've ever done. Being around Karen, makes me want to purge it all.

Giving in, I open my mouth to tell her just that, but then, my phone rings, snapping me out of my thoughts. Seeing Marcus's name, I quickly stand, and then say, "I have to answer this call."

Walking out of the room, I answer my old friends call, as I push down the uneasy sensation that's suddenly in my gut.

The instant I hear his voice, I glance back towards the door to our room, knowing everything is about to change. The only problem is, I don't know if it's for the good or the bad.

Chapter 11

Karen

The moment Jason walks out of the room, my stomach drops. I know whoever is calling him means something has happened. It's a sense, or maybe, it's more of instinct now. Either way, I can only hope my phone call to Riley hasn't done any more damage.

Letting out a sigh, I run both of my hands through my hair, wishing my racing heart would calm down. That kiss between Jason and I is still doing things to me. Even if I know I shouldn't feel this way towards him, I can't seem to help myself. Plus, I know I need to finally face how I'm feeling. Not to mention, it's a distraction from whatever hell awaits, once he's off of the phone.

Standing up, I pace in front of the bed, really thinking over everything that's happened recently. When I first met Jason, at Jake's Bar, I never once considered it would eventually bring me here in this moment. I never once thought I could fall in love with someone like him, or actually be okay with knowing all that I do.

That's what stops me from fully accepting it. I know what kind of man he is, I know he's done horrible things before me, and I know it's been while we've been together as well. But knowing all that I do, I still find myself falling hopelessly in love with him.

Does that make me a bad person, too?

Deep down, I don't think Jason is a bad person. He's made bad choices, but there is a part of him that wants to be good. I have to believe that not only for me, but for him as well. He's shown me that he can fight against the darkness inside of him, so why am I still fighting this connection we share?

Glancing towards the door, I let out a sigh, as I finally accept that I love him. There's no stopping it anyway, so why bother?

The moment I let it all in, my stomach fills with butterflies, as my heart races faster than ever before. I know better than to tell him how I feel, but I'm happy I've accepted it. Even if I might end up regretting loving a man like him later, I'd much rather go on knowing how I feel versus denying it.

The only problem now is the fact that I don't know how Riley is doing. I hate even thinking that I put her in more danger by calling her. Pacing again, I worry about her, and especially, her unborn babies. God, if anything were to happen to her, I wouldn't be able to accept it. I honestly can't even think about something happening to her, because if I do, then I'll remember the day I lost my older sister, Katie.

I'll remember how it feels to experience hopelessness, and how out of control it feels to not be able to help the one person you love the most in the world. That empty pit of nothing almost swallowed me alive, and I'm still surprised I survived. Katie's untimely death shaped me into the person that I am today, and the control I held onto so tightly afterwards was all I had left.

Jason showed me that the control I thought I needed to protect myself was nothing more than a façade. Control isn't real, at least, not in my case. I've been shown over and over again that the control I thought I had was nothing more than my way of protecting myself from everyone around me. But now, Jason is the one that holds the control.

I just have to fully trust him to keep me alive.

Pushing the thoughts of my sister and Riley out of my mind, I remind myself I can't keep dwelling on it. I can't keep holding myself responsible for things I had no control over. It's hard to let go, though. It's even harder than I realized to let someone else take over. However, it's easier to let it all drift away, knowing Jason will be there to pick up the pieces I can't bear to carry anymore.

Hearing the door shut behind me, I turn, seeing Jason walking back in the room. "What's wrong?" I ask, as I notice the look on his face. He looks broken, as if whoever called him, gave him the worst news imaginable.

"Jason?" I try again, as he sits on the bed. Sensing he needs me, I walk over, and then lay a hand on his shoulder. The moment his gaze finds mine, my stomach drops, as I suck in a deep breath. "What happened?"

God, those dark, brown eyes are so full of fear, and it shocks me to my core. "Dominic found my son."

My eyebrows raise, because I had no idea he even had a son. "Your son?"

"Julian," he states in a rough voice, and I instantly realize why he has that name tattooed on his chest. "I thought he would be safe, because I had a plan in place, when I left with you, but somehow, he's been found."

Bending down, I sit on my knees, as I say, "You said he's been found, not taken, right?"

He nods, and then claims, "I think Marcus got him out in time."

I frown, hearing that name, but I don't ask him about it. Right now, he's more concerned about his son, and he doesn't need me badgering him about people I've never heard of before. "You trust this Marcus guy," I state.

Jason nods, as he says, "I do. He's been by my side for decades, and I know he would do anything to protect Julian, even when I can't."

Grabbing both of his hands, I hold onto them tightly, as I claim, "Then we trust him now."

His gaze snaps to mine, and for a moment, neither one of us speaks. No words are needed at this moment, mainly because I can see his fear. I can feel it, as it comes out of him, hitting me right in the chest. Even if I don't know who Marcus is, I trust Jason's judgement on the matter.

I know if he's so shook up about the possibility of something happening to his son, then I know for a fact that he would never place his son's life in the hands of someone who would do him harm.

"Something has changed about you," Jason utters in a soft tone, and I glance away, feeling my face warm.

When I feel his finger under my chin, pulling me to look up, I swallow hard, and then remind myself to keep my emotions under control. Deep down, I know now isn't the time to tell him how much I care about him, or how much I love him.

He definitely doesn't need to hear that I would do anything to keep him safe.

"Tell me," he demands, and I close my eyes for a moment, letting the sensations of his demand flow through me.

All my life, I thought I was the more controlling and dominant one. I thought I was the alpha, which would explain why I had so many problems, finding the right guy. Turns out, I was just waiting for Jason.

Unable to help myself, I stop fighting the urge to follow through with his command. "Jason, I—"

"Jason, fuck! We've got to go. Right now."

Jumping, as Frankie's voice registers, Jason stands, and then pulls me off of my knees. "How many?" Jason asks him, and my stomach begins to turn.

Trying not to panic, I stand still, waiting for Jason to tell me what we need to do. "I saw two, but there could be more. They're lurking around the back of the hotel now, so I think we can lose them."

"No," Jason states, and I snap my gaze to him. Frowning, as he turns towards me, he cups my cheek, and then says, "Stay here, and do not leave this room, until I return."

Shock overwhelms me, even though I hear and understand what he's saying. Snapping myself out of the shock, I grab his hand, as he starts to leave the room. "Wait, Jason. You can't go. Please, don't go," I beg, because something is screaming that this isn't a good idea.

He could die for fuck's sake, and I can't even think about that.

I refuse to even consider it.

He must sense my terror, so he turns to face me, as he pulls me in close. Sucking in a deep breath, I wrap both of my arms around him, taking in his scent. The funny thing is, I can hear his heart beating, and instead of it racing like mine, it's a steady rhythm. There is no panic or fear in him at all.

He's calm and self-assured.

It's almost as if he's unbothered by any of this.

As he pulls me away from him, I gaze up, and then realize this is him in his element. This is the darkness that he keeps close by. It's not only to hurt others, but to keep me safe as well.

"Frankie will stay with you. I'll be back soon."

In a daze, I watch with wide eyes, as Jason grabs a bag, and then walks right out of the room. I don't move an inch, until the door slams shut, and for the first time in years, I want to let myself break down.

Fear is such a powerful emotion, and I can't seem to shake it off. No matter how hard I try to fight against it, I feel myself falling deeper into despair, unable to grab onto anything to keep me afloat.

If Jason doesn't return, then I know I'll soon follow him.

If he dies, it won't be long, before I meet the same fate.

Jason

I never imagined it would be so hard to do what I do best. It's not because these assholes are making it difficult. I'm actually surprised Dominic would send men this untrained, so it'll be easy to take them out.

It's hard to focus, because I keep picturing the utter terror on Karen's face, as I left.

That's not something I ever wanted to see, and now that I have, it's throwing me off my game. I've seen fear before, and it's never once bothered me. I've always done what I needed to get the job done, and then move on to something else.

As I fade into the shadows, I know it's different now, because it's Karen. Everything about this night is fucked up, and all I want to do is run. It's a little unsettling that I want to run, but I know I can't. There is no escaping what's happening, so I push down the sensation, and then let my inner beast come forward.

Rounding the corner, I spot the two men Frankie saw. I'm relieved that I decided to keep him nearby, and I'm even more grateful that he was here to give me a warning. Watching the two men closely, I quickly come up with a plan to get rid of them.

I'm going to have to eliminate them, even though I know Karen won't like that. It's too late to try and leave a false trail again. Not to mention, they'll spot us, if we were to try and leave now. They're checking the vehicles parked in the lot, and I wouldn't be surprised, if they started knocking on doors soon.

Crouching down, I open up the bag I brought with me, and then pull out my weapon of choice. Unfortunately, I need to be closer to get a clean shot, so I keep low, as I begin to make my way towards them. Thankfully, my thoughts clear even more, as I approach them, and it seems things will finally work out in my favor.

That's until a woman comes out of her room and spots me.

As soon as she lets out a scream, the two goons snap their gazes right to me, and I clench my jaw, knowing the element of surprise is long gone. Not giving the woman another glance, I jump up, and then race towards the men.

Everything around me seems to slow down, as I raise my hand, holding the gun, and the men do the exact same. Pulling the trigger, I don't even give the guy that falls down on the ground a second glance. I know my bullet hit right where I intended, so now, I focus on the second guy.

Swinging my arm towards him, I pull the trigger once more, but as soon as I do, he does the same.

Hitting my target again, I watch him tumble to the ground, and I know he's dead from where I'm standing.

However, I fall back against a nearby car, feeling a wave of intense pain. Letting out a groan, I look to where the pain is coming from, seeing the blood, pouring out of my left shoulder. Sliding down onto the ground, I let go of my gun, and then place a hand over the wound.

Clenching my jaw, I try to block out the overwhelming sense of pain, but no matter how hard I try, it's too much to handle. My vision begins to blur, and I shake my head, trying to stay awake. I cannot pass out right now. There is still so much I need to do to clean up this fucking mess, so I force myself to ignore the pain.

I have to, otherwise, it won't be Dominic who comes for me. It'll be the fucking cops, taking me to jail, and I can't let that happen. If I'm gone, then who will be there to protect Karen? Who will be there to get Julian, once all of this is over?

With the two most important people front and center in my mind, I lick my lips, and then pull myself off the ground.

After threatening the front desk clerk, he finally decides to give me the tapes from the cameras outside. I don't have time to see which ones I need, so I take them all, and then put them in my bag.

Knowing I need to get back to Karen, and then leave this hotel behind us, I hold onto my shoulder, making my way back to her. It seems to take longer than I realize to get back to our room, but I have to make it. We have to get the hell out of here, before the cops are called.

Finally, I make it back to the room, and it takes me a few tries to open the fucking door. Letting out a groan, I heave in a deep breath, as the pain intensifies. Thankfully, either Frankie or Karen must hear me, since the door flies open.

I stumble forward, dropping my bag, and then Karen is by my side. "What happened to you?"

"My arm," I mumble, unable to form a sentence to explain more. The pain is too much to bear, and I know I'm going to pass out soon from it.

"Frankie, help me lay him down on the bed," Karen commands, and I try to help them, as best as I can. My energy is almost gone, so I'm not much help.

"I need towels, Frankie. We have to stop the bleeding, so I can see what's going on." I groan through clenched teeth, as she begins to put pressure on my shoulder, and then she winces, once she realizes how much pain I'm in.

Once Frankie comes back with the towels, he hands them over to Karen, and then she uses them to soak up the blood, coming from my shoulder. The pain is almost unbearable now, but I push through it, knowing I need to stay awake.

"We need to leave," I grit out, as Karen presses harder on my wound.

"We need to get you fixed first," she counters. "I really could use a first aid kit," she adds a few moments later, and I clench my jaw, seeing the worried look on her face.

"In my car," I start, but then I stop to suck in a deep breath, before I'm able to finish. "There's one under the seat."

"I got it," Frankie claims, and then rushes off to grab it.

As he leaves the room, I reach over, holding onto Karen's hand. Her gaze finally finds mine, and I hate seeing the strain this is putting on her. "Tell me what happened, Jason."

"There's not much to tell," I confess, keeping her gaze.

She huffs out a sigh, and I know she's not happy with my answer. It's not that I don't want to tell her what went down, it's just that I don't want her to worry even more than she already is. I don't want to alarm her that the cops are most likely on their way, or the fact that I'm pretty sure the bullet is still in my shoulder.

After a few more moments of silence, Frankie returns with the first aid kit in hand. He quickly hands it to Karen, and she directs him to keep pressure on my wound. As she works, I fight the urge to give into passing out, and it's hard not to do so. Thankfully, it doesn't take her long to find everything she needs, since the first aid kit I brought with me, has more than the common kit does.

No words are spoken from any of us, as Karen uses bandage scissors to cut off my shirt, and then she and Frankie roll me to the side. Letting out a groan at the movement, I hear Karen's curse, as she realizes the bullet is still inside of me.

"We have to get the bullet out," she claims, and I nod, knowing it's going to hurt like a motherfucker. "I'll try to be quick."

"Here, take these," Frankie says, as he hands me two pills.

"What are you giving him?"

"Vicodin."

Glancing to Karen, I don't take the pills, until she nods. I know what Vicodin is, but I also don't make it a habit of taking anything like this. Narcotics tend to knock me out, so I know if Karen is okay with it, then things should be fine.

I just hope she hurries up, because it won't be long, before I'm literally out of it, and that won't be good for any of us.

Chapter 13

Karen

After Frankie and I manage to get Jason inside Frankie's truck, I head back into the hotel room to wash the blood off my hands. Reaching the sink, I stare at my hands, wondering how in the hell I managed to stitch up Jason without a second thought.

I'm not a trauma doctor, so I'm still shocked I got that bullet out, and then patched him up so quickly. Watching the blood wash away, I hope Jason will be alright. Worry is suddenly clouding my judgement, even if I know I did all that I could. Honestly, I would've preferred to take him to the ER, but I know that's not an option.

"Karen?" Turning towards Frankie, I push away all my conflicting thoughts. They aren't doing anything but driving me crazy with panic and worry anyway. "We should pack up and leave now. I also got rid of Jason's car, thinking it would be a good idea."

Nodding, I glance around the room in a daze. Knowing we need to leave, I begin to gather all of our belongings. It doesn't take long at all, and for some reason, it makes me sad. I miss my home and my things at my apartment. I wonder if I'll ever be able to finally go back to my old life. Glancing around the room again, I have a feeling, once all of this is over, I highly doubt anything will ever be the same. For some reason, I don't think I can just forget what's happened, or just go about my life like I used, too.

Deciding to worry about it, when the time comes, I walk out of the hotel room, and then get in the truck. Thankfully, Frankie opts to drive, and I'm grateful. I don't know this area as well as Frankie or Jason, so it makes sense for him to drive.

Turning around, I take a glance at Jason, and then sigh, seeing that he's finally let himself pass out. I know he was in a lot of pain, while I worked on him. It was clear in his eyes, but I also know he was trying his best not to show it. I bet he was doing it more for me than himself, but I'm glad he seems to be okay now.

As I face forward, I sneak a glance at Frankie. There are so many questions I want to ask him, but I'm not sure if I should. I don't know this person at all, but Jason seems to trust him. He has been helpful, so maybe, I should trust him, too.

After a few moments of silence, Frankie decides to break it. "You can ask me anything you want to know. I have nothing to hide."

Now that he's given me an opening, I take full advantage. "How did you get involved in all of this?"

"I owed Marcus, so when Jason called for me, I came." Frowning, I start to tell him that doesn't really explain anything, but then, he adds more, "I was a kid, when Marcus found me on the streets. I was in deep with a gang, and he helped me get out. I've been by his side ever since, and that's how I met Jason. I've done a few jobs for Dominic, but I'm not in as deep as they are."

Glancing back to Jason, I wonder if he'll ever tell me how he got involved with Dominic. I know there is more to his story, and I hope he trusts me enough one day to tell me everything.

"I know what you must think of me."

Snapping my gaze to Frankie, I claim, "I don't know anything about you to make any assumptions."

"That's true, but I'll bet you have some pretty bad thoughts about all of this."

Letting out a sigh, I look down at my hands, before confessing, "At first, I did." I glance out of the window, watching the street lights pass by, and then add, "Now, I don't know. I guess, I'm just not surprised by anything anymore. I've realized there isn't any reason to keep letting fear or panic rule my life, so I just take it day by day, dealing with whatever happens."

My gaze finds Frankie, as he says, "You're handling this a lot better than most would." I don't know how to answer him, so I stay silent. Honestly,

I'm shocked at how I'm taking all of this in, too. "He's not all bad, you know? Jason, I mean."

A small smile crosses my face, as I check on Jason again. He seems at peace in his sleep, and I hope he's getting some much-needed rest. Turning around, I state, "I know. I've seen the good in him, so I have to believe that he's not totally lost in his darkness."

"Marcus is like that, too."

"Tell me about him," I say quietly, hoping Jason doesn't wake up.

"There's not much to tell, but he's a lot like Jason. They're both protective of the ones they care about, and both will do anything to make sure they stay safe." Frankie turns into another hotel, and my stomach dips, thinking this will be how things are for a while.

As he parks, he turns to me, and then says, "Jason loves you."

I jerk back, shocked he would even think that. "No, he doesn't. He cares about me, sure, but I don't know, if he'll ever let himself love me." Giving Jason one final glance, I add, "I know what kind of man he is, and I've accepted that he might never feel love for me. I'm okay with that for now." Meeting Frankie's gaze, I claim, "I just need him to stay alive."

Once Frankie and I wake Jason, and then help him into our new room, Frankie leaves, saying he'll be close by. Thankfully, Jason seems to be in better shape than before. He did grunt a lot, as Frankie and I helped him in the room, so I can tell he's still in pain. At least now, he's actually sitting up.

Standing by him, I search for the words that I want to say. I'm not sure how to ask him what I need to, but after the talk with Frankie, I realize I need to know everything. I need to know every dark and twisted secret, if only to fully understand the man I'm in love with.

Before I figure out what to say, Jason stands, and I reach for him, as he sways forward. Wrapping my arms around him, he glances down at me, but he doesn't push me away, or utter a word. For a moment, our eyes hold, and my heart begins to race, as lust rushes through me.

"I need a shower," he states, as he surprisingly leans on me for support. Helping him to the bathroom, he sits on the toilet seat, as I get the water ready for him. It seems surreal that he's allowing me to help him, and I know he's letting me do this. Jason is a strong and proud man, so I know this chance wouldn't be happening otherwise.

Once the water is warm enough, I suck in a deep breath, as I gaze into his dark, brown eyes. The look he's giving me is more than just hunger and lust. There is need and … something else that I can't quite figure out.

Shaking myself out of the daze, I help him take off his shirt, being mindful of his shoulder. Dropping his bloody piece of clothing on the floor, I can't stop my eyes from taking in his muscular chest. Want and need are front and center, but I remind myself that he's still hurt. Needing a distraction, I check the bandage over his wound, hoping it won't get infected. A part of me is still in shock that he got hurt, and it's difficult to deal with the intense emotions, thinking he might have died earlier.

It's hard to even think about something awful happening to him.

When Jason's hand covers mine, I look at him, staring right into his eyes. "I'll be fine," he claims, and I give him a small smile. It's sort of off putting how he knows I'm still worried about him, but his reassurance is good to hear.

"How about that shower?" With his nod, he stands, and I only keep my hands on him to make sure he keeps his balance.

I also keep my grip on him, as he takes off his jeans, and again, I'm instantly wanting more from him. Maybe, it's because he could've died, and that makes my entire body crave him more than I ever have before. Maybe, it's also because a part of me knows that what's going on between us can't last forever.

How can we go on, knowing what awaits us, once all of this is over?

Snapping out of my thoughts, I can only watch, as Jason steps into the shower. Unsure of what I should do, I cringe, as he groans, when he tries to wash himself. Quickly undressing, I step inside the shower behind him, and then begin to wash him.

At first, he tenses, once he feels my hands on his back, but as I lather the soap on him, I feel the tension slowly leave him. I take my time, too, mostly because this moment is so rare, and I don't want to forget even a second of it.

Once I finish washing his back, he slowly turns, and I do the same to his front. I don't dare glance up, mainly because I'm afraid of what I'll find in his gaze. So instead, I keep my eyes on his hard and defined chest, enjoying the feel of his warm skin under my palms. As I make my way down lower, I smirk, seeing his stomach, jumping at my touch. I like knowing my touch does that to him, and it makes me feel powerful, even though I'm not the one who holds all the power in our relationship.

"You're not upset that I had to kill those two men?"

I frown at his deep and rough voice, but I'm not sure how to answer him. While I know he did what he had to, to keep all of us safe, I'm still saddened that he had to do it. "I don't want to talk about that," I say instead, hoping he'll drop it. I'm not ready to face exactly what he's done, even though I understand his reasoning.

Human life shouldn't be so easy to take, like he's done.

But nothing about this is black and white, like how I'm used to.

"What do you want to talk about then?" He asks, after a few moments.

"What makes you think I want to talk at all?"

He lets out a grunt, and then claims, "I can see the questions written all over your face." Clenching my jaw, as his finger touches my chin, I glance up, knowing he wants me, too. "I know you, Karen. So, ask your questions, and I'll answer them."

"Okay," I say, and then clear my throat, as I think of what to ask first. "How did you meet Dominic?"

When he doesn't immediately answer, I wonder if he's going back on his word, but then, he finally says, "My mother sold me to him, when I was fourteen."

I jerk back, because I'm shocked to hear his answer. "Sold you?"

He pushes out a deep breath, as he grabs the soap, and then lathers his hands. As he begins to wash me, I instantly relax, loving how his rough hands caress my body. "When I was eight, I watched someone murder my father. I was hiding, when the man broke into our home, but I still saw everything."

My stomach sinks, as I hear the remorse in his voice, but I don't dare speak. I know if I do, he'll stop talking. "Anyway, after Dad died, my mother wasn't the same. She got hooked on heroine, and Dominic used that against her."

He stops again, as he directs me to turn around, so he can wash my back. Once he starts washing me again, he continues. "So, when I turned fourteen, Dominic made her an offer that she couldn't refuse.

He fed her pretty lies, telling her he could give me a better life than what I had. I don't blame her for agreeing. Dominic knows how to be convincing, when he wants something, and I truly believe my mother thought he would honor his promise."

"But he didn't," I state, knowing I'm right.

"No, he didn't. His better life was to train me to become his greatest weapon." Turning back around, I hold his gaze, as he claims, "Dominic had my father murdered, so he could eventually bring me into his world. I didn't find out for a while, but once I put it all together, I asked him why."

"What did he say?" I prompt, when he stops talking for a few moments.

His jaw clenches, as he roughly says, "He told me that children are the future." With my frown, he adds, "I have no idea what he meant by that, and I still don't." Standing still, Jason brushes my hair out of my face, and then wipes away the water on my cheek. "Marcus was the one who was there for me, and he looked after me, like a brother would. He protected me from Dominic's wrath more than once, and I'll never be able to repay him for all that he's done."

"Is that why you trust him with your son?"

"Yes. Marcus hates Dominic just as much as I do, and he knows if Dominic ever gets his hands on Julian, he'll do what he did to many others before us."

When he goes quiet again, I reach up, and then cup his cheek. “He’ll be okay,” I say softly, knowing he’ll know I’m talking about his son.

He nods, and then says, “I know. He’s only five, but he’s a strong boy.”

As Jason turns off the shower, I claim, “You’re proud of him.”

“I am,” he says, as he steps out of the shower, and then helps me do the same.

We quickly dry off, and then dress, but neither one of us say anything else. He sits on the bed, and then I do the same, as I bandage his shoulder again. Once I finish, I let out a sigh, before I utter, “My sister died, when I was sixteen, because I couldn’t save her.”

Feeling his gaze on me, I keep mine straight ahead, as I claim, “She was at home swimming, and she somehow tripped, and then hit her head. She hit it so hard that it knocked her out, and she fell into the pool.” My heart races, as I talk about Katie and how she died. I haven’t let myself think back to that day, because I’ve always felt so guilty about it. Not to mention, how much guilt my parents made me feel every single time I was around them.

When Jason gives my hand a squeeze, I lick my lips, pushing down the urge to cry. “I came home not long after she fell in, and I immediately drug her out and started CPR.” Dropping my head, I close my eyes, as I croak out, “It didn’t matter what I did. She was already dead long before I arrived.”

My eyes burn with the tears that I refuse to let go of, because I know the moment that I do, there won't be any going back. I can't let myself let go of the pain or the hurt, since I know I'll never come back from it. The grief I felt the day Katie died was unbearable, so I won't allow myself to fall back into that dark pit of nothing but an emptiness void.

"Why do you feel so much guilt, Karen? It wasn't your fault. It was an accident," Jason states, as he cups my cheek, pulling me to look at him.

After a few moments of resisting, I finally give in and glance at him. "It was my fault. I was supposed to be there with her, but instead, I was out with some boy I liked. I should've been there with her. I could've saved her, if I had been there."

"Stop that," he demands, and I pull out of his grasp, as anger surges forward.

"Don't tell me how I'm supposed to feel." His jaw clenches, but all I can do is focus on the sudden anger I feel, rushing through me. I'd much rather feel rage than the intense wave of agony.

"Don't dare tell me it wasn't my fault, when I know it was." Jumping up, I shake my head, as I ask, "Just how many lives have you taken? Do you feel any guilt at all for knowing you caused their deaths?"

"I know you're upset right now, but don't ask questions that you really don't want the answers, too."

"Unbelievable," I utter, turning away from him. Running a hand through my hair, I turn back towards him, saying, "I do want to know. I want to know how you live with yourself, knowing what you've done." I have to know, because I can't keep on going, knowing I could've saved my sister. If he tells me how to live with the endless guilt, maybe I can live with it, too.

However, instead of answering me, he narrows his eyes at me, as he stands, towering over me, and I suddenly feel the sexual tension between us. I hold my breath, as he leans in close, and then whispers, "If you're looking to fight with me, I'll give you a fucking fight."

Jason

Staring at Karen, I know she's hurting. I know she's holding onto the pain of losing her sister, but fuck, she's pushing me too far. There is only so much that I can take, before I push back, and that's exactly where I am now.

The things she's asking of me, I can't give them to her.

No matter how much I want to tell her the truth, she's not ready for it. She may think she is, especially since she's so full of anger, but I know her better than she knows herself. Listening to her story about her sister, it just confirms what I've always known about her.

The control she thought kept her safe isn't real. It's made up in her mind, and it's just a stupid emotion to make her feel alright. I also know deep down, she's still grieving. She's still hurting from losing someone she loved so much. I can see it, but what I don't get, is why she doesn't. Why is she still trying so hard to push me away, and to make it clear she's the one in control?

Well, I'm about to remind her pretty ass that I'm the one in charge here. I'm the one that will carry all her pain and anger. This is what I was made to do, and I know this is why I met her, when I did. It wasn't just because Dominic ordered me, too. I fully believe Karen was made for me, and *only me*.

"What do you say, vixen? Do you really want to do this?"

"You won't hurt me," she claims, but her voice breaks, and I know she's nervous.

"No," I state. "I'll never physically hurt you."

She frowns, as she asks, "What does that mean?"

"I'm going to break down all those fucking walls around your heart, and I'm going to make you see that you need me more than either one of us realize." Stepping forward, I wrap my hand around her throat, and pull her closer to me. My grip isn't tight at all, but it's to show her I mean business. "I will own you in every way possible. I want your body, heart, and even your soul."

Hovering right over her lips, I smirk, feeling her pulse, racing under my fingertips. Her eyes start to close, and I know she's feeling exactly what I am. Fuck, I want her so badly, and if I don't have her soon, I might lose my fucking mind.

"You will give me what I want, vixen."

When she licks her lips, my cock jumps, wishing I had her pretty lips wrapped around my cock. Just thinking about her on her knees, makes me want to come, but I push down the urge for now.

"Make me," she utters in the sexiest voice I've ever heard, and I smirk, silently accepting the challenge.

Before she can pull away, I take her lips, and instantly devour her. She doesn't put up a fight, as I push my tongue deep inside her mouth, and I realize I'm done being gentle with her.

If she wants the beast, then I'll fucking give it to her.

My hand around her throat tightens, as I use my teeth to bite her bottom lip. Her breathy moan makes my cock harden even more than before, and I realize how much we both need this.

Using my other hand, I slip it under her shirt, and then cup her breasts with my palm. As she arches her chest towards me, I pinch her nipple, enjoying her whimpers. I take my time, teasing her, and I know she's ready for more, when she places her hands under my shirt.

Pulling away, her eyes flare with desire, and then she licks her lips. I can't bear to look away from her pretty mouth, because I'm becoming obsessed with everything there is about her. Guiding her to her knees, I'm surprised she does so without defying me. Maybe, her need is just as strong as mine. Maybe, she wants this to happen just as much as I do. Either way, I'll make sure she knows how proud I am that she's complying.

As soon as her knees hit the floor, her hands are instantly on my pants. I stand still, as she frees me, and I clench my jaw, once her hot and wet mouth wraps around my cock. She sucks me hard and deep inside her mouth, and I grab a hold of her hair, urging her to pick up the pace.

So lost in the pleasure she's giving me, I almost miss her, slipping a hand into her pants. Jerking her head back by her hair, I bark out, "Don't you fucking dare."

She groans on my cock, and the vibrations make me want to come. Holding back the urge to let go, I pull her away, and then help her stand. Her eyes are glazed over with need and lust, and I smirk, loving that look on her.

"Take off your clothes," I order, and she instantly does so.

Unfortunately, the moment I try to do the same, my shoulder screams in pain. Karen is quick to come and help me, and for just a moment, I feel something rush through me. I'm not quite sure what it is that I'm sensing, but whatever the emotion, I realize it's strong, and I actually like it.

When she runs her hands down my chest, my heart starts to race. The tenderness in her touch is almost too much to handle, but I let her continue, because I know this means something more to her, too.

However, my need for her grows, and I'm done with the gentleness.

Taking her by her wrists, I back her up, until her legs hit the bed. Guiding her to lay on her back, I'm quick to hover over her, while I keep her hands above her head. It's a little difficult to use my other arm, since it's beginning to hurt again, but I ignore the pain.

I want her too much to stop now.

Reaching down, I slowly use two fingers, as I push them inside of her tight pussy. I groan, as she arches her chest, and I feel just how wet she is for me already. As I begin to tease her, I relish of how she feels around my fingers, and how vocal she is, when I do something she loves.

Right as she's about to come, I take my fingers out of her, and then take her mouth again, when she lets out a moan in complaint. Shoving my tongue deep inside, I feel as if we're both on the edge of no return. Our kiss is so full of passion, but it's like we're both desperate for more.

Pulling away, I don't hesitate, as I use my hand to help guide my cock inside of her. I can't seem to look away, as I watch her pussy take me in, and a surge of possessiveness flows throughout my entire body.

"You're mine, Karen, and don't you ever fucking forget it," I state, as I slide all the way inside of her.

For a moment, I hold still, so she can get used to me, and because being inside of her feels a lot like coming home. I know this is more than sex or about me dominating her. What we have, it's something I never knew I could have. This connection we share will never just go away, simply because we're surrounded in death and destruction.

"Jason, please," she says in a breathy tone, and I know she wants me to move.

Giving her exactly what we both want, I fuck her hard.

I don't dare hold back, and I don't stop, until her voice is hoarse, and we're both spent.

Waking up the following morning, I frown for a moment, realizing Karen is right next to me. After getting my fill of her last night, I let sleep take me under, and I completely forgot to handcuff her to the bed. As much as I hate to keep having to do so, I assumed she would run again. Now, I see it's not needed any longer.

She could've left me last night, but she didn't.

She stayed right by my side.

Pride rushes through me, and my chest tightens, seeing how content she seems. Brushing her hair out of her face, I slowly get up, and then make my way to the bathroom. Quickly taking care of my needs, I walk back into the room, and then let out a sigh, seeing her still sleeping. I don't bother waking her yet, because I know she needs the rest. These past few weeks have been stressful for me, so I can only imagine how it's been for her.

Hearing my phone chime with a text, I give her one final glance, before I grab my phone off the table. My stomach knots up, seeing Frankie's name, but I remind myself it could be good news. I'm still waiting to hear from Marcus, and hope blooms in my chest, thinking Frankie might know what's going on. I have to believe Marcus and Julian are safe and okay, or I might lose my mind with worry. There isn't a moment that passes that I'm not thinking of my son, and I hope I'll be reunited with him soon.

When I read the text from Frankie, I clench my jaw, knowing our time here in Texas is up. With my mind made up, I send him a text back, letting him know to stay here and keep an eye out for any signs of trouble, while Karen and I go to Mexico. It's always been the plan to go to my cabin in Cozumel, but I didn't think it would be this soon.

However, Isaac making an appearance close by, is fucking with the plan.

I should've known he'd eventually figure out who I was, and I knew Riley would want either him or Conner to come looking for Karen. My short time with them taught me many things, and most importantly, how loyal they all are with each other. As much as it pisses me off that Isaac is meddling in my business, I have to also remember why he's doing it. I know they're worried about Karen, but I won't let him take her back.

Dominic is still out there, waiting and watching them, so Karen will stick by my side, as long as there is danger.

Putting my phone in my pocket, I quietly pack our bags. That way, once Karen is awake, we can immediately put Texas behind us. It'll take a few hours to get to our final destination, so it's smart to leave, as soon as possible.

Once I finish packing our things, I walk over by Karen. For a moment, I watch her sleep, wishing our situation were different. Honestly, I would've never met her, if it hadn't been for Isaac and Conner's past, or them meeting Riley. It's by pure chance that I came into her life, and that has to mean something. No other option is acceptable, so I have to believe somehow, somewhere, there is a force, pulling me to her.

As much as I hate who I am, I can be better for her. I have to be better for her, because if I'm not, then I don't deserve to even be near her.

"Karen," I say softly, and then rub her arm, trying to wake her. "It's time to go."

She groans, but she does roll over, and then opens her eyes. "What time is it?"

"It's early, but we need to go."

As she sits up, she nods, and then gets up to go to the bathroom. I sit on the bed, as I wait for her to finish, and end up convincing myself it'll be best not to tell her Isaac is nearby. Hell, it was one hell of a coincidence that Frankie spotted him, but I'm glad for it. If Karen knows he's here, then she'll want to go home with him, and I can't allow that to happen. A part of me knows that it's not right to keep even more things from her, but like I said before, I can't chance her getting hurt in Dominic's fucking games.

"Where are we going this time?" She asks, as she walks out of the bathroom.

Seeing no reason to lie to her, I answer, "Cozumel, Mexico." Her eyebrows raise, and then I add, "I have a place there, and we'll be safe. No one knows I own it."

"Why didn't we go there first then?"

Standing, I walk over by her, and then cup her cheek, as I claim, "I needed to be sure no one was following us there." When she leans into my touch, my chest tightens again, but I don't think too much about it. It's hard to think about anything else, when she is around. "It's okay for us to go now, and I promise we'll be safe there."

"Okay, I trust you," she says softly, and hearing those words coming from her, makes my heart begin to race.

I never once thought she would trust me, not after all that I've done, but yet, here she is, giving me her trust willingly. Leaning down, I can't help myself from getting another taste of her, even if I had more than enough of her last night. It seems I'll never have enough, so I greedily take all I can.

Deep down, I know something will eventually happen that'll take her from me. Whether it's someone else, using her against me, or maybe, it'll be me that does it.

Maybe, I'll wake up one day, and then realize, all of this was nothing more than just a dream.

Karen

I can't seem to control my excitement, as we make our way to Jason's cabin. All this time that we've been running, I hadn't realized how much I miss seeing other people. It's surreal, seeing the locals walking or riding their bikes in the small town in Mexico.

It's amazing how much you miss, when you don't have it right at your fingertips anymore.

My eyes take in every little detail I can, as we pass by, and when the colorful buildings are left behind us, I turn towards Jason. His hand tightens its hold on mine, and I smile, liking how he's being so gentle and tender with me.

While I very much enjoy the demanding side of him, I find that I like this side, too. It shows me that he cares enough to be this way with me, because I know he can be hard and rough most of the time. A part of me wonders, if he's trying harder to be sweet now that we're in a safer area. Either way, I'm committing every bit of this to memory.

As we turn down a dirt road, I frown, and then sit up straighter in the car. I don't see any signs, letting me know exactly where we are, but I know Jason has all of that covered. He wouldn't bring us anywhere that he hasn't been before. It's good to know that he knows the layout of the area, too. It's comforting to trust him just in case we need to make a quick getaway.

"We're almost there," Jason claims, and my stomach fills with butterflies, hoping we're going to be near a beach. I can see the water from the car, and I would love to be able to put my feet in the water again.

Not long after, he parks the car in front of a small cabin, but it looks more like a hut or a bungalow. It seems cozy from the outside, and I quickly get out of the car, wanting to see more of it. Palm trees stand tall beside the cabin, and I instantly kick off my shoes, feeling the white sand, touching my feet. It's so warm from the sun, and I let my head fall back, as I feel the warmth on my skin.

I'm also glad that I was right about a beach being nearby, too. Hearing the waves crashing against the shore, I grin widely, and then turn towards the sound. Seeing all the locals by the water, I watch them, as they go about their day. There are also a lot of people on their boats or jet skis, enjoying the nice summer day.

Feeling a hand, wrapping around my waist, I lean my head back against Jason, seeking more of his comfort. "We can go down to the beach, once we get settled in."

Looking up at him, I ask, "Promise?"

He caresses my cheek, as he states, "Promise. I know how much you love the beach, so whatever you want, you'll get it."

Smirking, I don't dare tell him how much I like hearing that. Instead, I say, "Thank you for bringing me here. It seems so peaceful, and I'm surprised you don't stay here all the time."

"Maybe one day," he utters, as he drops his hand from my face. My chest tightens, hearing the sadness in his voice, and I wonder if he thinks he'll forever be tied to Dominic. "Come, I want to show you the inside," he quickly says, and then takes me by the hand.

Following him inside, I take in the small cabin, finding I really like it here. Even though it's small, it doesn't feel cramped at all. The sitting area and the bedroom are in one big open area, and there is a kitchen to the right. Seeing a door closer to the huge canopy bed, I assume that's where the bathroom is located.

I take my time walking around, making sure to touch everything. I'm still surprised we're here, and that Jason claims it's safe for us. I have no doubt that he's telling me the truth, because he wouldn't put us in danger on purpose.

"What do you think?" He asks, and I glance back at him, smiling widely.

"I love it. I just might move here, when all of this is over."

"Good," he claims in with a smirk. "How about you change into your suit, while I unpack, and then we can go to the beach."

Nodding, I rush over to him, and then wrap my arms around his neck. Leaving a kiss on his lips, I try to hold back a laugh, seeing his expression. Pulling away, he licks his lips, and then watches me intently, as I grab my swimsuit, before walking into the bathroom.

Once there, I let out the laugh I was holding in. I never thought I'd see the day that I could shock him, but it happened, and I vow to make sure that look happens more often.

It would do him some good to relax more.

Laying back on the towel, I soak up all the rays of the sun, while enjoying the sounds of the waves, crashing against the shore. I know we've been out on the beach for quite some time, but Jason hasn't uttered a word of complaint. He's not as relaxed as I am, but I'm glad he's here with me.

Not that I had much of a choice to be by myself.

I tried to get him to rest, especially since I had to do some more doctoring on his shoulder, but he was adamant about staying by my side. I eventually gave him what he wanted, knowing it would ease his mind.

Feeling his gaze on me, I glance at him, and then smirk, seeing the desire in his eyes. "You should take a picture. It'll last longer," I tease.

It does what I want, and he smirks, while shaking his head. As he leans in closer, I suck in a deep breath. It never fails to amaze me how quickly my body is turned on, when he's near. "Keep teasing me, and I'll fuck you right here on the beach."

Swallowing hard, I find I wouldn't mind that at all, but then, a couple walks by, reminding me we're not alone here. "You'd really take me in a public place?"

He pushes out a breath, and then stands, before saying, "No, I don't want anyone seeing what's mine."

Taking his outstretched hand, I ask, "Possessive much?"

"Don't act like you don't like it." Raising an eyebrow in defiance, his gaze darkens, as he claims, "You're just asking for another spanking." Before I can say anything to that, he adds, "Come, it's getting late, and I want to cook dinner."

Reaching down, I grab the towel, and then place my hand in his. "You do remember I don't cook, right?"

"Yes, I'm very aware that you can't cook." I take no offense to his flat tone, because I know it's the truth. "I think you're the only person I know that can burn water."

Letting out a laugh, I state, "It's a gift."

"I'm not letting you cook tonight, so don't worry."

"Good, because I would feel really bad, if I burned down your cabin," I say, as we walk inside.

Jason shakes his head, but I see the happy glint in his gaze. He likes my playful banter, and I like seeing him so at ease. "Go change and shower. I'll be in the kitchen waiting," he states, and then smacks me on the ass.

I narrow my gaze at him, while he stares back with hungry eyes. Knowing what that look means, I make sure to give a little shake of my hips, before walking into the bathroom.

As I turn on the water, I undress, and then try not to let myself worry about Riley. It's frustrating that I can't just call her and make sure she's alright. I hate being kept in the dark, but I also understand why Jason won't allow me to make the call I need.

I just have to hope that my friend is alive and safe.

Once the water is at the right temperature, I get in and let the hot water sooth my muscles. The ache reminds me of last night's fun with Jason, and how much I want to experience that pleasure again. I'm not sure how he does it, but he always knows exactly what to do to make me crave even more from him. It's like I'm addicted to him, and everything he has to offer.

Quickly washing myself and my hair, I hop out of the shower and dry off. It's strange that Jason isn't in here with me, and honestly, it feels weird. Maybe, I'm getting used to him being around me all of the time, since he hasn't left my side much, after he took me.

Which is why, I hurry to dry my hair and to get dressed. How can I miss him, knowing I just left him? Am I developing some sort of separation anxiety? Whatever the case, I instantly relax, as I walk into the kitchen, seeing him chopping up something on the cutting board.

I watch him for a few moments, before he finally turns around. I'm not sure if he sensed me or what, but when our eyes meet, it's like something in both of us snaps.

Taking a deep breath, as he turns off the stove, my heart begins to race, as he makes his way over to me. What is it about him that makes me want him this much? The need he brings out of me is kind of scary, but I don't really dwell on it.

All I can think about is him approaching me, like a predator stalking its prey.

Once he reaches me, he instantly cups my cheek with one hand, as the other slides into my hair. Holding onto him by the waist, as he kisses me with abandon, I melt into him, knowing there is no point in denying him what he wants.

It's pointless to fight anymore, while I know I want the same exact thing.

Pleasure.

A little bit of pain.

And most of all, I want to feel our connection.

As Jason takes me hard and fast, and then soft and slow, I wonder if maybe Frankie was right. I wonder if he really and truly does love me, but he just doesn't know how to tell me.

Laying on my side, I gaze at Jason, admiring his perfectly sculpted body. He's so handsome, and it's hard to look away. He doesn't seem to mind me ogling him, but after a few moments pass, he turns on his side, facing me.

As he reaches forward, I hold still, when his fingers touch my lips. It's such a tender touch, and once again, I'm surprised by it. When he pulls away, I move closer, wanting to feel his warmth against my skin.

We stay like this for a long while, before I notice something change in his gaze. It catches me off guard for a moment, because the look he's giving me now, is like he's angry, but at the same time, he's not. It's as if he's in a deep thought, and I wonder what has him so lost inside of his mind.

Reaching over, I caress his cheek, as I ask, "Where did you go?"

He blinks a few times, before finally focusing on me again. I start to ask him once more what's on his mind, but then he says, "I never told you about Julian's mother."

I choose not to say anything, so he'll keep talking, because I'm curious about the woman who caught his attention enough to have a baby with him.

"Her name was Rachel, and I met her by chance, while on a job for Dominic." He sighs deeply, as if this memory is hard for him to talk about.

Giving him time, I make sure to keep touching him, urging him to finish telling me the story. "It was supposed to be a one-time thing, but she reminded me that there was a better life than the one I was living. So, I kept going back, even though I knew I shouldn't have."

"Eventually, she found out who I was and what I am," he states, and the tone of his voice makes my chest clench. It's like he doesn't think he's worth anything, but what Dominic made him in to be. "Needless to say, once she learned the truth, she didn't want to see me anymore. I understood, because I didn't want to put her in any danger, so when she disappeared, I never gave it a second thought."

His gaze holds mine, as he adds, "Dominic found her a year later. I hadn't known it at the time that he was having her followed."

"Why would he do that?" I ask, and my stomach twists, because I have a feeling I already know the answer.

"She had just given birth to Julian, but I had no idea she was even pregnant."

"She ran to keep your son safe," I add, and he nods, confirming my suspensions.

In a gruff and a hard tone, he says, "Dominic wanted me to choose between them."

"What do you mean?"

"I had to pick which one would live and which one had to die." His jaw clenches, as he claims, "Dominic always had a sick way of doing things to make sure we all stayed in line, and I think he knew who I would pick."

When he sits up, I grab the sheet to cover myself, as I wrap my arms around his back. "I couldn't kill my son. I couldn't even imagine taking a life of such an innocent little thing, so I did what Dominic wanted. Even if I know I had no choice in the matter, I still carry that guilt with me every single day. There is nothing I can do to change what I've done, so that's why I swore to keep Julian away from all of this chaos. Marcus helped me the first year, but then, Dominic finally got arrested and went to prison."

"Because Isaac and Conner testified against him," I add, knowing this part of the story. It's the only reason how the District Attorney was able to fully convict Dominic, and then gave him such a long sentence to make sure he stayed in jail.

It's a shame that he somehow was able to escape prison.

Jason nods, and then says, "It was pure luck, when it happened, but Marcus and I were glad for it." He goes silent for a few moments, and I hold him tighter, knowing he has more to say. "When word got out that Dominic was out, I told Marcus to take Julian. I have no idea where they went, because I was worried Dominic would try to make me tell him where they were. So, it was best that I didn't know anything."

"I hate not being with my son, and I hate Dominic still has a hold over me. I think that's another reason why he had Rachel followed, too. He knew if she ended up pregnant that he would have some type of leverage over me."

Closing my eyes, I let out a sigh, as I state, "He wanted you under his control no matter who paid the price."

"Yes, he did. Dominic put a lot of time into making me how he wanted me to be, so it makes sense that he'd do whatever was necessary to keep me contained."

I hate hearing him talk about himself, like he's a tool or a machine. There is so much more to him than just a heartless man, and I decide right then and there, that no matter how much evil he's done, I'll stay by his side no matter what.

If I don't, then the good in him will never fully surface, and I can't let that happen. Even if I know he's done a lot of bad things, I can't just sit by and let him fall completely into the darkness.

I'll be the light that keeps him right where he's needed.

Jason

The only thing that's keeping me from disappearing into the dark void is Karen's touch. I focus on her hands, and how good they feel against my skin. I take in everything about her and hold onto it, as tightly as I can.

Talking about what I did to Rachel was harder than I thought it would be. It's hard to remember the fear in her eyes, especially when she realized what kind of hell she'd been brought into. There isn't a single day that goes by that I don't regret what I had to do, but I couldn't let my son die.

It was the hardest decision I had to make, but I know I made the right one.

I just hope Karen doesn't hate me for what I had to do. That's why I told her the truth. I knew holding that key piece of my past back was a mistake, so I wanted to get it all out in the open. I honestly wouldn't blame her if she wanted to leave me now.

Although, I would try and convince her to stay for a bit longer.

Turning to face her, I cup her cheek, as I state, "Now, do you understand what kind of man I am?"

Surprisingly, she leans into my touch, and I frown, as she says, "I do know, Jason. You're not the monster you think you are. Yes, you've done some awful things, but you know what else I see?"

My heart begins to pound in my chest, as I take in her words, hoping she's not lying to me. I have to believe that she's being completely honest, otherwise, I don't think I can take it.

"I see a man who is trying to be a better person. I see the good you're trying to do, and I know you feel guilt and remorse for those horrible things. That's what makes the difference. How can you be a bad man, when you hate what you were made to do?"

"Please, don't make me into some sort of saint, because I'm not," I state forcefully.

She rolls her eyes, and I smirk, liking how she's still defying me without even realizing it. "I'm not doing that at all, Jason."

Brushing her hair out of her face, I sigh deeply, as I ask, "Do you remember what you asked me, before we came here?" With her frown, I add, "You wanted to know how I live with myself, knowing what I've done." With her nod, I finally give her the answer she needs to hear. "The guilt never goes away, and I believe it'll always be there."

When she looks away, I know she's thinking about her sister. It wasn't hard to figure out why she asked me that, because she still blames herself. Using my hand, I caress her cheek, pulling her to look at me again.

"It does get easier to carry it, but you have to forgive yourself for what happened. I'm not saying it'll happen overnight, but one day, you'll be ready to accept what happened, and then be able to move on."

With a shaky breath, she whispers, "I don't know how to do that."

Pain unlike anything I've ever felt before, rushes through me, but I'm not surprised by it. It's because she's hurting, and there isn't anything I can do about it. Her pain isn't something I can just fix, even though I wish I could.

"It'll take time, but you have to face what happened, and then fully believe you were not at fault for it."

After a few moments, she nods, but I know it'll take more than this conversation to get her to see that. When she's ready, she'll be able to let go of the pain, grief, and most importantly, the guilt.

I just hope I'm there for her, when it happens, because it won't be something she needs to go through alone.

While Karen finally lets herself drift away, I stand outside on the small porch, taking in the cool air. I can't seem to relax enough to let sleep take me, even though I know I need the rest. I just can't shake the feeling that something is about to happen.

I know we're safe here, because I made it so. No one knows I own this place, since it's not even in my name. *So, why can't I shake away this unnerving sensation?* It's like my instincts are screaming at me to move again, but that could just be, because we've been on the go so much. I'm so tempted to call Frankie, and check to make sure things are okay, but I refuse to do so. If something happened where he is, then he would've called or texted me by now.

Running a hand through my hair, I push down the uneasy sensation, and then turn to walk back inside. Right as I place my hand on the doorknob, I hear someone calling my name. Clenching my jaw, I hold still, because I know that voice.

I know that voice, because I've heard it so many times, while Dominic was plotting his revenge.

Dropping my hand, I glance through the window, making sure Karen is still asleep in bed. Once I realize she hasn't moved, I turn to face the son of a bitch who is either insane, or he has a death wish. "How did you find me, Lance?"

He shrugs his shoulder, and that's when I notice the gun in his hand. I have to give it to him, he at least came prepared. "It was difficult to find you, but you should've known we'd eventually figure it out."

through with it. Grabbing my phone instead, I head into the bathroom, and then dial Frankie's number.

It rings once, before he answers. "Frankie, I need you to come to me. How fast can you get to Cozumel, Mexico?"

Karen

I wake to a cold and empty bed the next morning, and I instantly know something isn't right. Glancing around the room, I don't see Jason anywhere, so I get up and quickly get dressed. My heart pounds in my chest, as I look for him, and then fear begins to creep up, when I finally spot him outside.

As I make my way towards him, I wrap my arms around myself, seeing Jason and Frankie, talking in a hushed tone. *Something is wrong, I just know it*. Right before I reach Jason, he turns, and the look in his eyes makes my stomach drop.

"What now? I thought we were safe here."

He doesn't answer me right away, and instead, he turns towards Frankie, and then says, "Give us a minute."

With his nod, Jason takes my hand, and then leads me back inside of the cabin. As we stand in the seating area, my heart races, as I wait for him to tell me what's going on. "Jason, please. Just tell me," I state, knowing it'll be better to just get it out there.

"I have to go back."

"Go back? Go back where?"

When he begins to pace, my panic raises even higher. It's clear that whatever has happened is bad, and I know he's trying to work through it. Giving him the time he needs, I try not to rush him into talking. I know whatever is going on isn't going to be good, but I wish he would just tell me, because we *can* handle it.

Together.

"One of Dominic's men came to see me last night."

"I need to sit for this," I claim, and then all but fall onto the couch. I can't believe, while I was sleeping, Jason was with someone that could've killed us both, and I would've never known.

"I have about forty hours to return, before they kill Julian."

Jerking back, shock and confusion race through me, as I work through this new information. "How do they have Julian?"

"I have no idea, but they do. I was shown proof of it, and I can't let anything happen to him."

"I understand that, but why do they want you so bad?"

Jason shakes his head, and then runs a hand through his hair, as he claims, "To use me, Karen. That's all I'm fucking good for anyway."

Jumping up, I take his hands in mine, as I state, "No, that's not all you're good for, and you know it."

He stares at me, like I've suddenly become a stranger, and the look he's giving me honestly scares me. "Dominic is dead, but that doesn't matter. His son is in charge, and he's not too happy that I'm not around." I bite my tongue, when he pulls away, and then turns around. With his back facing me, I feel as if he's purposely shutting me out, and it hurts to know he's doing it.

"How did they find us?" I ask in a soft tone, knowing he's on edge right now.

"Dominic's son is a fucking police detective, so he had everything at his disposal to find not only me, but my son as well."

My legs suddenly feel weak, so I opt to sit back down. This shit just keeps getting even more insane with each second, and I don't know how much more of this I can take. "What are you going to do, Jason?"

"I have to go back," he claims, and then he turns to face me. "I have no choice, but to do what he wants, or Julian will pay the price."

As soon as the words leave his mouth, Frankie walks inside, and then my stomach drops. "Why is Frankie here then?"

"He's here to take you home, Karen."

Glancing back and forth between them both, I frown, and then say, "I thought it wasn't safe for me to go home."

Jason drops his head, as he claims, “I don’t think you have anything to worry about now that Dominic is dead.”

“But this detective must know about me, right?”

He shakes his head, but then, he finally meets my gaze. “He might, but either way, you have to go home. I can’t have any other distractions right now.”

My eyes widen, as his words flow through me. I’ll admit, it hurts to hear what he’s saying, even if I understand why he doesn’t want me around anymore. “I don’t want you to do this, Jason.” The sick pit in my stomach is telling me this is a horrible idea. “There has to be another way to get to Julian, instead of you having to go back to that life.”

“There is no other way,” he sternly states, and my chest clenches, knowing I’m losing this battle with him. “They will kill him that I have no doubt of, so you’re leaving with Frankie. I don’t care if you don’t agree, but it’s going to happen with or without your consent.”

I narrow my eyes at him, and then I stand, glaring right into his dark eyes. “If I don’t want to go, then I won’t. Nothing you say will make me leave you right now. Jason, you need me, and you know it.”

His jaw clenches, and for just a second, I think he might just relent on this. But then, his eyes dart to Frankie, and before I realize it, something stabs me in the arm. Looking down at the sensation, shock and disbelief rushes through me.

That son of a bitch drugged me.

Again.

Snapping my gaze back to Jason, I sway, and then fall back. My eyes begin to drupe, as I realize Frankie is the one who caught me. I don't know why, but knowing it wasn't Jason, really puts the sting in rejection.

"I'm sorry, Karen," Jason says softly, as he caresses my cheek. "There is no other way."

Right before I lose the battle to whatever sedative he gave me, I utter, "I hate you."

Jason

Helping Frankie place Karen into the car, I shut the door, hating myself even more than I already do. I didn't want any of this to happen, but Karen gave me no other choice. I knew she wouldn't willingly leave my side, so drugging her was the best option.

I can't let her distract me anymore than she already has.

If she's by my side, there is no way I can do what needs to be done.

"Are you sure about this?" Frankie asks, as he walks over by me.

Nodding, I order, "Stay by her side at all times, just in case this detective gets any bright ideas."

"Will do." My chest clenches, as Frankie walks over to the driver's side of the car, and I realize this might be the last time I ever see Karen.

Placing a hand on the window, I stare at her sleeping form, wishing, yet again, that things could be different for us. Meeting her, has been an eye opener, and I don't regret it for one second. Our lives are just too different for this to work, and I finally accept that.

I just hope that she does the same, once she's back where she belongs.

"I knew you'd make the right choice," Lance claims, as I approach him.

I don't dare say that I didn't have much of a choice on the matter, and he must know it. The sick asshole grins widely, as I get inside the car, and I will myself to stay calm. It's hard to do so, since I know I'm literally being forced to go back to my old life.

Deep down, I knew this moment was coming.

The kind of man that I am, there is no escaping the hell I've lived. No amount of good will ever erase all of the evil I've done, so it's best to just accept the path I've been given.

In the end, if I can protect the ones I care for, then I have to believe all of this is worth the price I'm having to pay. My soul is tainted, and I know I'll have to carry the burden all on my own.

Chapter 19

Karen

One week later

Standing in the middle of my studio apartment, I sigh, feeling as if I don't belong here. It's a strange sensation, but the moment I arrived with Frankie, it's been here. It's a constant reminder that things will never be the same, after all I've been through.

It's a constant reminder that Jason has changed me, and I can't seem to find my way back.

Maybe, I'm rushing myself to go back to normal. Maybe, I won't let myself be who I used to be, because if I do, what happens if Jason returns? I have to hold onto hope that he'll find his way back to me. I can't even think about being without him, so every night, I lay awake in bed, wishing he were next to me.

Pretending has become my new normal.

It's easier to think things are fine, even after a week of being back home. The thing is, my home isn't here anymore. My home is with a man that is most likely out there doing unspeakable things.

"Hey, Kiki? Can you hand me a towel?"

Turning around, I immediately slap my hand over my eyes to block out the sight of Frankie, standing outside the bathroom totally naked. "Really, Frankie?"

"What? I forgot my towel."

"Obviously," I sarcastically state. Keeping my eyes on the floor, I grab him a towel, and then toss it to him. "When are you leaving?"

I know Jason ordered him to stay by my side, since Frankie admitted so, once I woke up in the car. While I appreciate the extra security, I'm not sure rooming with him is going to work. Frankie and I are two completely different people. He's a slob, while I like my place neat and organized. He sleeps all day, while I like to wake up early. The list of our differences can go on and on, but at least, he's still here and didn't abandon me.

"Are you so ready to get rid of me?"

Letting out a sigh, I take a chance, and then glance over to him. Thankfully, he has the towel wrapped around him, but I still don't know how to answer him. Yes, I want him gone, because he's driving me crazy, but then again, I don't want him to leave.

He's the only link I have to Jason.

If he leaves, I fear that'll be the final straw to me losing Jason forever.

Instead of admitting any of this, I opt for indifference. “Well, if you’re going to stay, then you should at least start cleaning up after yourself.”

“Yes, Mother,” he states, and I glare at him. “I like being around you, Karen. It’s the most fun I’ve had in a long time.”

Shaking my head, I walk into the kitchen to grab some takeout menus. “Just remember who buys your food every single day.”

“Oh, speaking of food,” he claims, and then rushes by my side. I swear he could eat all day long, if I had the money to feed him so much.

Once we decide on what to eat, Frankie walks towards the bathroom to change. “Hang up your towel, when you’re done,” I call after him.

His response is to drop the towel, showing me his ass. Groaning, I quickly turn around, and finally realize why some siblings argue and fight so much.

“I don’t know why you have to be with me just to grab food right around the block.”

Frankie shrugs, as if it’s common to follow someone around, as much as he does me. “I think you know why I do, but let’s pretend I do it, because I have a crush on you.”

Rolling my eyes, I smack his shoulders, knowing very well he’s joking. “I’m sure by now things have calmed down enough, so you can go back to your home."

"I don't have anywhere else to go," he says in a soft voice, and my chest clenches, hating to hear the pain in his tone.

Not knowing what to say, I follow him upstairs, leading to my place. Glancing down at my feet, I suddenly feel my chest clenching. Letting out a breath, I try to shake off the sensation, because I know why I'm feeling this way.

I miss Jason, and I'm worried about him.

I have no way of knowing if he's okay, or what's going on. I hate being kept in the dark, but I understand why he's keeping his distance. As much as I wish he could check in, I know he's still trying to keep me safe.

So lost in my thoughts, I bump right into Frankie, as we reach the apartment door. "What's wrong?" I ask, once I notice how tense his entire body seems.

"Someone broke in," he states, and I glance up, seeing someone did break in.

The door to my home is wide open, and there are bits of wood on the floor from where the person kicked it open. Panic threatens to rise up and take over, but I remind myself I'm safe with Frankie. This could just be a random occurrence, because it's not unheard of, but then again, what if it isn't?

What if this is the work of the man that made Jason return to his old life?

"Stay here," Frankie claims, and I grab his arm to stop him.

"No, you can't go in there. They could still be in there, waiting for us."

"I'll be fine," he says, and then pulls out a gun that I hadn't known he was carrying.

Pushing out a breath, I let go of him, and then watch with wide eyes, as he disappears into my apartment. It seems like so much time passes, while I wait for him to return, but I do as he ordered. It's hard to stay where I am, but I'm not stupid. If someone is still inside, it's smart to stay outside that way I can make a quick getaway if necessary.

Just as I begin to lose my patience, Frankie walks towards me. "No one is here, but it doesn't look like a normal break in."

"How do you mean?" I ask, and then we both go inside.

I glance around my place, looking for anything that could've been taken. Nothing seems to have been touched, and confusion begins to race through me. "Whoever broke in, just wanted you to know that they were here."

"None of this makes any sense," I utter. Running a hand through my hair, I gaze at Frankie, as he tries to shut my broken door. "I think I should call the police just in case."

With his nod, I pull out the new phone I purchased the moment I got back, and then make the call. Once I finish, I set my phone down, and then take a seat on the couch. After a few moments of silence, Frankie joins me, and then asks, "Are they coming?"

"Yeah, they'll be here soon."

As soon as the words leave my lips, there's a knock at the door. Standing, I frown, and then walk towards the door. "That was fast," I whisper, as I try to ignore the sudden unease I feel in the pit of my stomach. Sensing Frankie behind me, I relax a little, knowing he'll be here to protect me. Hearing knocking again, I jerk open the door.

"I'm Detective James, and I'm here about the break in."

Stepping back, I let the detective in, but something about him seems familiar, and at the same time, makes me stay alert. My heart begins to race, as I watch him, looking over my apartment, but I don't understand why I'm getting such a bad vibe from him.

"That was some quick response," Frankie claims, and I nod, thinking the exact same thing.

Detective James shrugs, as he says, "I was in the neighborhood."

Staying close by Frankie's side, I wonder if he can sense the sudden tension in the room. There is something about this man that is dangerous, and I wish I knew what it is that's making me think this way.

"Nothing was taken?"

"No, but the door was busted open, so we just assumed someone broke in."

"So, neither one of you saw anything out of the ordinary, before you entered your home?"

"We had just gotten back from grabbing food," Frankie cuts in, and I'm grateful for it. I'm not sure I can handle being around this detective much longer.

"Are you Karen Keens?"

Tensing, as Detective James says my name, I lay a hand on Frankie's arm, since I notice him, reaching for his gun. "Yes, that's me."

"And you know Riley Blake?"

Something inside of me is literally screaming at me to run, but I force down the sensation, as I ask, "Why would you want to know that?"

"She reported you missing a few months back, so I'm sure she'll be happy to hear you've returned."

As Frankie tenses, I quickly say, "It was just a misunderstanding. I went to stay with some family." I don't know why I lie to him, but I feel like I need to. I just can't shake that there is something more going on here.

Detective James nods, and then begins to walk around my apartment, as if he's scoping the place out. "Do you have family in Texas then?"

"I'm sorry Detective," Frankie cuts in. "What does her whereabouts have anything to do with someone possibly breaking into her home?"

Before Detective James can answer, there is another knock on the door. This time I hear a voice, letting me know who is behind it. Feeling a bit safer, knowing another police officer is here, I quickly make my way over towards the door, and then open it. The man instantly says his name is Detective Scott, and I lead him inside, completely confused as to why there are now two detectives in my home.

After a few intense moments and glares between the two detectives, Detective James finally leaves, and the moment he does, I push out a heavy sigh. God, that man freaked me right the hell out.

“Miss Keens, I don’t want to take up much of your time, but I need to know a few things.”

Nodding, I ask, “What do you want to know?”

Thankfully, Detective Scott gets straight to the point, as he asks, “How long, after you reported the break in, did Detective James arrive?”

“Not long. Frankie and I thought it was strange to have someone respond so quickly.”

“Did he ask you any strange questions, or threaten you in any way?”

Glancing towards Frankie, I don’t answer, until he gives me a subtle nod. “He didn’t threaten us, but something is off about him. He also asked if I knew someone, and I’m pretty sure I’ve seen him before.”

“Where have you seen him?”

Running a hand through my hair, I really think about where I’ve seen Detective James before. Now that he’s gone, and I have a moment to let myself think, and I do just that. Thankfully, Detective Scott gives me plenty of time to figure out the puzzle.

“He worked on a case involving my friend a few months ago,” I blurt, finally realizing how I knew him. He was the detective that worked on Riley’s ex-girlfriends murder case, and the one that was involved in the whole Dominic shit. As soon as I put it all together, my eyes widen, as I realize something very important.

"Is there anything else you'd like to add?"

"No," I instantly answer, because I can't say this without knowing who I can trust.

Detective Scott clenches his jaw, but he must realize I'm done talking. "Here's my card, if you can think of anything else."

Taking the card out of his hand, I stand still as a statue, as he leaves. Once the door shuts, I sag, as I let out another sigh. "What was all that about?" Frankie asks, but I don't answer him, until I'm sitting.

Still holding the card, I keep my gaze on it, as I ask, "Do you remember Jason saying Dominic's son was a police detective?"

"Yeah, I do, but what does that have to do with any of this?"

Looking up at him, I claim, "I think Detective James is Dominic's son."

Karen

Frankie doesn't utter a single word, once I tell him what I suspect, but I think he knows I'm right. "Why else would he ask those things about where I've been, or even about Riley? It's just too strange to chalk it up as a coincidence. Plus, it would make sense if it is him, because how else would he know where I live? What if it is him, and this is another way to control Jason?"

"I believe you, Karen."

Dropping the card, I run both hands down my face, as I say, "This is all so fucked up."

"Listen, Karen," Frankie says, as he walks towards me, and then bends down. "If Detective James is Dominic's son, then we need to be very careful. He could have people watching us now, so we both need to stay alert."

"That's not helping my stress, Frankie."

"I know, and I'm sorry," he states in a soft voice. "Neither one of us is safe anymore, but I know Jason and Marcus will have a plan. They'll take care of it."

Staring into Frankie's eyes, I see he does believe what he's saying. I wish it were that easy for me. I wish things weren't so fucked up, and more than anything, I wish Jason were here.

However, I've learned very quickly that wishing for things isn't going to help me at all.

One week later

Another week passes, and there has been no word from Jason.

A part of me hopes that it means things are okay, and that he's still alive. However, the other part whispers it's because he's dead, and I wouldn't even know it.

It's been difficult to go about my life, as if I'm supposed to just forget everything I know, or what all I've seen. It's hard knowing that a fucking police detective could be the sole reason why I don't have Jason here by my side.

Since Frankie has been around, he's helped me keep my mind off of not only Jason, but Riley as well. No matter how badly I want to talk to her and let her know I'm okay, I just can't seem to follow through. There are several reasons why I haven't got in touch with her, but the main reason, is because I'm just not ready to face her.

So, for now, I pass the time by watching boring TV shows with Frankie. Today, I'm not sure what garbage he's picked, since all I can do is stare at the screen blankly. "Hey," Frankie says, as he bumps my shoulder.

Glancing at him, he grins, as he says, "I bet I can get you to smile."

I roll my eyes at him, but it's nice he's trying to take my mind off Jason and Riley. "I'm not in the mood for jokes today."

He stands, and then says, "Well, if you change your mind, I'm here all day."

Letting out a snort, I realize he's not wrong. Neither one of us have left the house, since the break in. I don't even go to the lobby to check the mail anymore. Thankfully, Frankie does it for me. Watching him, as he walks towards the door, he winks at me, before doing the daily task.

Reaching for the remote, I shut off the TV, and then grab my phone. I pull up Riley's number, but I don't call her. Biting on my thumb nail, I really consider the risks of reaching out to her. I know she'll be happy to know I'm alive and well, but what if that detective is waiting for me to call her? What if he's having her watched still?

No matter how I'm feeling, I have to keep her safe.

So lost in my thoughts, I jump, when I hear the door shut. "Sorry, it's just me," Frankie claims, but I notice the understanding in his gaze. We've both been on edge lately, but who could really blame us?

"Anything good?" I ask, as he hands over the mail. Glancing down at the stack, I quickly toss the bills and junk mail to the side, but there is one letter that catches my attention. Holding it up, so Frankie can see it, I ask, "Do you know who this is from?"

The white envelope only has my name on the front, and the handwriting isn't from anyone that I recognize. "I'm not sure," he says with a shrug.

Dropping my gaze back to the letter, I open it, and my eyes widen, as I realize who it's from. With a shaky voice, I utter, "It's from Jason."

"That's good. Now, we know he's alive," he deadpans. It seems I'm not the only one, hating the radio silence.

Getting off of the couch, I make my way towards my room, as I claim, "I'm going to read this in private."

"Yeah, that's probably for the best," Frankie says right as I shut the door, leading to my room.

Sitting on the bed, I just hold the letter for a bit, while I let myself enjoy the sensation of knowing Jason is alive. Looking down at it again, I suck in a deep breath, as I realize he must have stuck it in my box, since there is no address. The thought of him being so close makes my heart race, but it also sends a pang of loneliness through me. I hate knowing he was close by, but yet, he didn't come see me.

I guess he thought things weren't safe enough to risk it. It's the only thing I can think of as to why he wouldn't just walk up one flight of stairs, and then knock on my door.

Pushing down all the mixed emotions, I unfold the letter, and then begin to read it.

Karen,

I know you must be angry at me for the things that I have done, and the most recent one, by making you leave. I hated to drug you, but I also knew you'd never leave my side, if I hadn't. I'm only doing what I thought was right, because I thought sending you away was my only option. I can't have you getting hurt, because of the choices I have made.

There are things I need to tell you, and things that I need you to understand. This problem I have gotten myself in, it will not go away easily. Things are about to get worse, before they get better, and I need you to trust me. There are going to be things I have to do, and you are not going to like them. I can't tell you what my plan is yet, or whether I'm coming back or not, because I refuse to give you false hope.

My main priority is to get Julian far away from Vincent, and then take him down. Which means, I need you to stop waiting for me to come back. I know your life has changed drastically, but you have your freedom back to

do with whatever you wish. I need you to go on with your life, and not stop living, because I'm not around.

I also want you to know that I'm still fighting the darkness inside of me. It's a lot harder without you by my side, but for you, I will continue to fight for as long as I can.

I don't know what path lies ahead for me, and I have no idea how any of this will play out. Just know, you're always on my mind, and there isn't a moment that I'm not thinking of our time in Mexico.

Stay safe, Karen.

Keep Frankie close.

Jason.

Dropping the letter onto my lap, I run my hand through my hair, as I process all this information. It's hard to think that he's going through so much, knowing he's alone. There is no mention of Marcus, so I have to think he's dead.

My chest clenches, just thinking about it, and what Jason is having to do.

Carefully folding the letter, I stand, and then walk over to my dresser. Placing it safely inside a drawer, I take comfort in knowing I can always read his letter again, when I'm missing him.

However, he's right about one thing. I'm still waiting for him to come back to me. As much as I don't want to admit it, I want to be here, if or when he returns. I hate that I don't know what's going to happen, and I hate not having control over the situation.

I just have to trust Jason will do everything in his power to make sure he stays alive, and then, when it's safe for him, he'll make his way home.

To me.

Epilogue

Vincent

"Lance, we need to do something about Detective Scott. He's been snooping around too much, so I need you to follow him and learn his routine. I want to know everything there is to know about him."

Looking up, when I don't hear an answer from him, I raise an eyebrow. "Yes, sir," he quickly says, and I tilt my head to the side, enjoying the fear in his eyes.

"Good. Now, get the fuck out of my office."

Watching Lance leave, I smirk, liking how he's quick to obey orders. *Like the good dog he is.*

I know Lance will get the job done soon, because Mason Scott is starting to become a pain in the ass. I never thought he would cause so many problems with him only being at the precinct for a few months, but from the moment him and I crossed paths, he's been a thorn in my side. I wish I could slice the chief's throat for letting that nosey bastard transfer here.

However, I'm going to hold back the urge to do so, since it could backfire on me.

Everything was going according to plan, until Scott started looking into my old case files. I still don't know why he isn't convinced, like everyone else that I'm the perfect cop, but then again, maybe it's my own fault for not forging the report better.

I still blame my father for killing Cammie Turner. If he had just listened to me, then I wouldn't be in this situation. Lighting a cigarette, I know soon enough I won't have to worry about Mason Scott any longer.

Lance has no choice but to come through, especially after I broke into Karen's home. Thinking back to that day, I should've held back the urge to see the woman that Jason choose. She must have something special, since she's made Jason almost worthless.

However, I can't deny that she's a looker.

Just thinking about her, makes me wish I had her locked in my basement, waiting for me. I bet she would be a fighter, and I do love a good fight, before taking what I want. Adjusting myself, as I think about how fun it would be, I push down the sudden need to take her for my own.

Rolling my chair back from the desk, I walk over to the window. Jason should be here any minute now. Surprisingly, he didn't put up much of a fight, when I sent Lance after him. Although, I'm sure knowing I have his son is motivation enough. I hate having that little brat here, but it's necessary to keep Jason in line.

My father was smart to find and then train him to be the perfect killer, and I can use that to my advantage. I don't fully know why my father wanted Jason as much as he did, but as long as he keeps doing what he's told, I won't kill him. *Yet.*

Walking over to the table to my right, I grab the scotch, and then pour a drink. As I take a drink, I relish the burn, as it goes down my throat, and then finally, settling in my stomach. Hearing the door to my office open, I turn, seeing Jason walking in.

"Is it done?"

The rage coming off of him makes me smirk, because he hates that I have the one thing that'll keep him in line. *He hates that I have power over him, but I fucking love it.*

"Yes, he won't be a problem anymore," he claims in a rough voice.

"Good. Now, I have another task for you."

His jaw clenches, but we both know he'll do whatever I say without a word. "I want to see Julian first."

Shaking my head, disappointment rushes through me. I should've known he'd pull this bullshit. "May I remind you that if you don't do what I ask, I'll have him killed, before you can even blink. I need to be able to trust that you won't just take him, and then run."

I love seeing the defeat in his eyes, because he knows I've won, and if he knows what's good for him and his little shit, he'll do well not to question me again.

When Jason doesn't utter another word, I walk back over to my desk, and then open the drawer to remove the file I have for his next victim. Tossing him the folder, he wastes no time, looking it over. He can deny it all he wants, but he loves the killing just as much as I do. I can see his eyes light up with excitement, as he carefully looks over the information.

"You have twenty-four hours to get the job done. Now, get the fuck out of my office."

He says nothing, as he walks out, slamming the door behind him. *Such anger*. He has no idea what I have in store for him.

Everything is going just how I imagined it would. There is still the problem of Isaac, but I can wait a little longer for that plan to work out. I might just wait, until Riley has those brats of hers, and then take them in as my own, since it seemed to work out well for my father. Who knows, maybe I can make my own little empire of vicious killers.

Dominic always said children were the future.

I sigh, thinking about how I had to kill the old man. I wish he could be here with me now to see how everything is turning out so great. It'll only continue to get better, once Lance gets me the information I need on Mason. After I take care of that problem, I'll be home free.

Taking another drink of the scotch, I sit down, and then plan out what comes next.

This is going to be so much fucking fun.

The End

Acknowledgements

Okay, I'm going to get a little sappy for a moment. I have so many amazing people to thank, but I don't want to forget anyone. Instead, I'm making this thank you for all of you. Firstly, I would not be here, doing what I love, if it were not for you, the reader. Thank you for taking a chance on me. I honestly don't have enough words to express how grateful I am for you wanting to read my books. I hope you love it as much as I did, while writing it, and thank you again from the bottom of my heart for reading.

Secondly, to the wonderful ladies in my fan group. Thank you for sticking by me, when things weren't going so well. Thank you for keeping me sane, and for all the laughs. Thank you for the naughty posts, as they were highly appreciated. You guys are absolutely amazing, and the love and support each and every one of you show me, is awesome. Ladies, you keep me going, and for that, I cannot thank you enough.

Thank you to my talented cover designer. Arijana, you made this cover look so amazing and beautiful.

A huge thank you to my editor, Nikki. I honestly can't thank you enough for all your hard work. I really appreciate every single thing you do for me, and not just as my editor. Your friendship means the world to me, and I love you, babe.

Linda, you're such a great new asset to my team, and I'm so grateful to have you. Thank you for your hard work, and most of all, your honesty.

Last but not least, thank you to my husband. All of your support will never go unnoticed, and everything you do to help me complete a book. Thank you for giving me the free time, when I need it the most. I appreciate all that you do for me, babe.

Other Books by Brie Paisley

Worshipped series

Worshipped-book one

Redeemed-book three

The Harlow Brothers Series

Carter-book one

Caden-book two

Caleb-book three

Carter and Shelby: Ever After (coming soon)

Standalone Novels

Temptation

Addiction

Brie Paisley was born and raised in a small town in Mississippi, and now, she currently lives in different locations, due to her husband being military. She wanted to write at a young age and was always filling journals with her thoughts and short stories. Brie started with an idea for her debut novel a few years ago, and with the encouragement of her husband and sister-in-law, she was able to write and publish her first book. When she isn't writing, you can find her reading a good book, watching a good movie, or spending time with her wonderful husband and beautiful daughter.

Facebook: @authorbriepaisley

Instagram: @authorbrie_paisley

Twitter: @author_brie

Printed in Great Britain
by Amazon

74505823R00098